THE LOST DARLING

BAILEY BLACK

Enjoy!
xoxo
Bailey Black

Edited by: Magnolia Author Services

Proofread: Alexandria James, Lucy Kosakoski, Ashleigh Blakely

Beta Readers: Alyssa Friess

Cover: Maria Spada

Publisher: Baileybbooks

About

Second star to the left and continue until morning.

I got that line tattooed on my wrist the day I turned twenty-one. So much symbolism in such a simple sentence. At the time, it was a nod to the future and the infinite possibilities to come, while reminding me to remember the past and to look for magic in the world.

Growing up, nothing was ever what it seemed. The shift of leaves on a tree was a faery skipping by. Shooting stars were a chance to make wishes. Shadows were souls stuck between this world and the next, mirroring a life they once had.

My imagination was limitless, the world a wonderful adventure waiting to unfold.

It's easy to lose that sense of wonder with the weight of life on your shoulders, and I wanted a reminder to get me through the hard days.

Most importantly, it was an ode to the boy who earned the title of my first crush, even if he was animated. Peter Pan wasn't a *save the damsel* kind of prince. He was daring, and selfless, and took care of the ones he loved. He was a friend to all but never afraid to fight the Pirates when their moral compass broke. Wendy was an idiot for leaving him. She rushed home to a heartless world full of men willing to lie through their teeth to get down her pants.

But that's the beauty of a book, the characters are perfectly flawed. Damaged just enough that we still love them. Whereas reality is nothing but empty promises and baggage the size of mountains.

The day I got my tattoo I would have given anything to be whisked away into a fairytale. My world was crumbling and all I wanted was to go back to when life was simpler. I didn't realize I had sealed my fate in ink.

Branded myself as one of The Lost.

Neverland was everything the stories made it out to be. Beautiful. Full of magic. Filled with handsome men and debonair pirates. But the author of my favorite tale left out one crucial detail.

In order to get there, you have to die.

CHAPTER 1

Wednesday

Three drinks down and I am convinced this bartender has magic hands. She's found a way to mix rum and a dozen other concocktables together until it tastes like a liquid dessert. Her sweet, pineapple slice of heaven is exactly what I need to forget the utter shit-storm my life has become in the last six months.

I pull the mini umbrella out of its ice bath and place the Maraschino cherry between my teeth and pop the stem. I close my eyes and suck on the little round fruit until all the flavor has faded away, then bite down. The cherry alone is a treat but paired with whatever else is in my cocktail, chef's kiss.

A few more rounds, mixed with the spritzers I drank earlier, and I might be able to forget that I walked in on my sister six months ago, legs spread, my boyfriend's hands cupped around her perky double-d's, while she bounced on his cock. Unlikely, but with every ounce of alcohol I swallow I get that much closer to temporary peace.

"You okay there, Wens?"

The simple answer? No, but life hasn't been simple for a long time. I open my eyes and smile at Kierra, my sister's maid of honor, the liquor lifting my lips even though I'm beyond pissed.

My sister broke her pinky promise. That was supposed to be my job. I should be the number two in command.

I was supposed to help plan this weekend's festivities, picking which booze cruises we went on during the day and which bars we bounced to after dark. I would have made sure she had a spotlight dance at the strip club we went to last night and kept boobs-McGee from drinking too much and causing a scene because that's the maid of honor's job.

Instead, I'm just the sister of the bride. Not even a bridesmaid in the wedding or a ridiculed adult flower girl. I'm a guest with a pity invite to the bachelorette party.

I'm the reject.

The girl the bride was forced to bring along that pretty much everyone ignores.

Tyle—said sister...twin sister... who is getting married in two weeks to my ex-boyfriend—and I have been planning our weddings since we were innocent, star-eyed ten-year-olds who found Leonardo DiCaprio back in his *Titanic* days on cable tv. That man was fine as sand during the late nineties and has only gotten better with age. He made me realize I had a thing for the preppy, blonde-haired, blue-eyed, heart-throbs.

And my sister had a thing for what was mine.

"I. Am. Peachy." I take another sip through the paper straw in my cup (hate those) and frown when I pull more air than yummy good-ness. I feel like my glass is broken, possibly with a hole in the bottom.

So was the one before that.

And the one before that one too.

I hold the empty drink up, signaling the wizard behind the bar that I'm ready for another round of her signature drink, a kiss me on the lips.

I have no shame in ordering it, but I wonder how many guests our bartender has honored with its name. I bet her drink makes for some great tips and even better stories.

If I were working behind the bar, I'd be kissing every hottie that ordered one. Male. Female. Unicorn. It doesn't matter anymore. A broken heart has made me open to all sorts of things I never thought I'd do. If it's not illegal and will make me forget the searing pain in the center of my chest, I'll try it.

Right now, our bartender has her eyes set on a tall drink of broody goodness, probably deciding if he's worth a little lip-locking. I vote yes, but there's no telling what this chick is into. For all I know, she may have a vag badge. Not hating that prospect, she's a gorgeous girl.

I fight a smile. Tyle would have a fit if I kissed a girl this weekend. She's still living in the past when it comes to relationships.

As much as she deserves to have her perfect weekend ruined (in her eyes kissing the wizard would cause waves) I'm trying to be good.

That's what family does. They respect each other. Even if my sister doesn't know what it means to leave well enough alone, I know my place.

Kierra takes the scalloped glass from me and sets it on the bar top, a concerned frown on her face. She stares at me for an uncomfortably long amount of time. I don't know what she expects to come out of my mouth.

Venom about the wedding?

Curses to her name for stealing my job?

If that's the case, she's going to be sorely disappointed because the one thing I'm not gonna do is give Tyle a story by making waves. That's the ocean's job. Mine is to cruise through this weekend in a drunken haze and make it to Monday morning.

I hiccup and cover my mouth with my hand, laughing in between each breath of air.

"You should go back to the boat and get some rest." Kierra took on the role of mom for the group this weekend. I should be grateful. Without her intervention last night, I would have ended up with so much more than another tattoo on my forearm. Nipple rings were *this* close to happening. I'm grateful for her presence, but I'm still mad at her.

She helped my sister not pick oleanders for the table decorations.

She didn't suggest the sweetheart, A-line gown that hugged Tyle's curves in all the right ways.

And she didn't talk my sister out of sleeping with my boyfriend.

Or marrying him.

Although, if I'm being fair, by the time Kenny proposed to Tyle, I couldn't claim him as mine anymore. Whatever. It's all semantics. Either way, my sister is marrying my ex six months after our breakup and it's fucked.

"I'm fine." I hiccup. "I just need another one of these." Hiccup. I reach for my glass, but Kierra slides it out of reach. I frown at her, ready to give her a piece of my mind, when the wizard appears again.

"Here you go, honey." Our bartender sets another delicious piece of heaven in front of me.

I snatch my drink before Kierra can steal it away. I don't know how the bar babe saw me, but I don't care. I'm grateful. Memories I'd rather not relive are burning through this haze of alcohol and I need to extinguish them. "What do I owe you?"

"Nothing." The chick steps back and tilts her head, signaling down the bar. "That gentleman bought it for you."

"Oh!" I say as Kierra murmurs my name—Wednesday—in a warning tone.

The bartender steps away, turning her attention back to paying customers. A temporary moment of disappointment that she wasn't the one who noticed me is replaced by a flicker of excitement. This whole weekend, all eyes have been on Tyle.

This is the first drink someone outside the wedding party has bought me. I'm not gonna waste it or an opportunity to talk to a hot guy.

Tall, dark, and broody stares at the flat screen above the bar. There's a football game playing, probably a re-run, but he seems interested in it. Tattooed fingers curl around a tumbler of amber liquor, bringing the glass to his lips as he studies the screen.

I take a sip of my yellowy-orange-goodness and smile against the straw. It's heaven in my mouth. Just like the other three. Or was it four? I don't know, and it doesn't matter. My goal is to stay numb this weekend, and this man is helping me reach the finish line. The fact that he's eye-candy is an added bonus.

Kierra grabs my arm as I slide out of the stool. The sheer white cover-up I have over my bright red bikini slides down my shoulder, exposing sun-kissed freckles. Tyle took after our mom. Her natural brown hair, before she bleached it, was four shades lighter than mine, her lips fuller, waist smaller. I look like our dad. Darker. Thicker and just... more.

"What are you doing?"

I shrug and back-step away from Kierra. She doesn't try to stop me, probably because she knows the effort is futile. Considering all the things I've almost done this weekend, me talking to a guy is the least of her worries, but it doesn't keep her from scowling as I creep away.

"It's only polite for me to thank the sexy stranger." I flash Kierra a grin we both know too well. It was Tyle's go-to back in the day when she was up to no good. I don't know what my plans are for this dude.

Probably nothing more than a little shameless flirting, but knowing that Kiera will tell Tyle and that Tyle will be jealous makes me happy.

A few tiny waves won't hurt anyone.

"Wens..." Kierra warns again.

"Relax, *Mom*. I'm just gonna say thank you. Maybe chat him up and get some more free booze. What's the worst that can happen?"

CHAPTER 2
Wednesday

I'm nervous.

Which is stupid because the guy who bought my drink isn't even that hot.

Okay. That's a lie.

He's kind of gorgeous.

Tattoos of twisting designs and symbols I've never seen before cover his arms, chest, and down to the band of his black bathing shorts, while his defined back has a giant map of a tropical-looking island. There's not a spec of color in the art. Just shades of gray and black against copper skin and deep-set muscles.

He's got a nineties-style fringe, where the hair is short in the back but falls over his brows in a sexy just-been-fucked kind of way. His eyes, a blue that parallels the deepest parts of the ocean, hold mine as I approach. He knew I'd come. A quick upturn of his lips against his glass confirmation of my suspicion. He doesn't look at me. His gaze is fixed on the flatscreen above a shelf of liquor, but I can feel static building between us the closer I get.

I lean against the bar and try not to puke as I smile. My nerves are running rampant, like a teenage girl with a crush in my system. It's been years since my heart stuttered this fast. If this dude was blonde, it would be game over. I wouldn't even try to fight my needy lady bits. I'd give in, right now, in the single-stall girl's bathroom down by the pool and screw him until my legs don't work right. But his hair is dark and I haven't had that much to drink yet. So logic still has some say in my life.

"Hi." My head spins from the rush of adrenaline. I take a sip of my drink, using the cool liquid to ground my body. From afar, he was beautiful, but up close, he's an anomaly cut from marble. This man is too pretty to be real.

And he's looking at me.

Not Tyle.

Me.

My sister wasn't far, just six seats down the bar chatting with a random man she met on the boat. It would have been nothing for tall, dark, and broody to look past my plain brown hair and boring hazel eyes. Tyle's bleached blonde strands and big blues have a way of luring men into conversation. Mr. Broody wouldn't have been the first to buy her a drink today, which could be why the cocktail was sent to me.

I push back the fear sneaking into my thoughts. Guys have always noticed Tyle first and used me to be by her side.

My ex—Kenny—was the only man I knew to choose me over her. She could have had him in high school, when she threw herself at him. Literally. Naked on the trampoline at a party after graduation. But he left her there, sloppy and crying (because she lives for the drama), to come find me.

Tyle had always been everything I wasn't, even when we were younger, but when Kenny and I were together, I was more than enough. Someone noticed me. Wanted me. I was on cloud nine until my world came crashing down. In what felt like an instant, I wasn't good enough for him anymore.

I wonder if that's the predicament Tyle is in now. If Kenny has grown tired of her but is in too deep to let go. If so, I don't feel bad. Karma is a bitch and her retribution is more than deserved.

It would explain why Kenny and Tyle gave each other a hall pass this weekend. They decided that what happens at the bachelor and bachelorette party stays there.

No questions.

No regrets.

One last hoorah.

I take another sip of my drink. The mental image of Tyle ruining my brand new couches creeps into my mind again. Only this time, Kenny's scarlet hair is as dark as night, his face replaced by my new friend's.

I feel sick again, but this isn't a nervous kind of sick. It's a heart hurts, gut-retching, reminder that the man I loved chose my sister kind of sick, mixed with the dark thoughts that I will never be good enough.

Don't get me wrong, I am still pissed at both of them for the betrayal, but I know I did nothing wrong.

Outside of never granting backdoor access, I gave Kenny anything he wanted. I was everything a girlfriend should be, sometimes even more, but the insecurity of not being good enough has embedded itself in my DNA. It's morphed into a passing thought every time someone looks at me. Most days I can silence the clamor with a drink. Others I can barely look at myself in the mirror.

Today I'm choosing to drown the voices.

Today I refuse to let Tyle win. This may be her weekend, but it's my life. If I want to get blackout drunk and hook up with a stranger I will because I am enough! Cheers to me!

My hand moves faster than my mouth is ready for and some of my drink spills over the rim of the glass and onto my chest. It's cold and the flimsy coverup does nothing to keep the sticky liquid from dripping between the girls.

"Shit," I mumble.

Tall, dark, and broody chuckles. The rumble of his voice vibrates deep in his chest and somehow has a direct connection with my lady bits. The poor girl has finally woken up after a temporary celibacy streak and set her eyes on this unfortunate soul.

"Allow me." He grabs a handful of bar-squares and presses the small white napkins to my chest.

Sober, pre-broken hearted Wednesday would have taken a step back to excuse herself, clean herself up, take a mini bath in the sink, then dry her tits under the hand dryers. She would be embarrassed and probably sneak away when no one was looking, then go home and fantasize about what could have happened had the stars aligned.

That version of me disappeared one heartbreak and two drinks ago.

This newer, freer me likes the heat burning through the napkin from Mcbroody's touch. And she ain't stopping him. He runs his fingers across my collar bone, between the peaks of my breasts, and down near my belly button, until his rough calluses grip my hips.

8

I forget how to breathe, every fiber in my body is set alight with need, and I let out a laugh I banished when I hit puberty.

"I missed a spot." He leans closer, oblivious to the embarrassing noise I made. His tongue swipes against the sensitive skin at my neck, nowhere near where my drink spilled.

I'm not complaining.

Desire spreads from my center, lighting me up from head to toe. It's exhilarating. I haven't felt this good since... no. I'm not thinking about the dickhead who broke my heart right now. Not when this man is making me feel So. Good.

"I think I got it," Mcbroody whispers in my ear. He pulls his lips away, just far enough for me to turn and look at him.

There's a brief moment between us, one where static bounces and electricity cracks. It's barely a second. Just long enough for me to back away if I don't want this.

But I do.

Oh, god. I do.

I see it in his eyes the moment he gives in. The man without a name growls, the feral sound deep in his throat, then devours me. His lips find mine, hungrily taking everything I have to offer and then some. Our tongues dance together, roaming, exploring, fighting for dominance. One hand cups the back of my neck. The other fists the sheer material of my cover-up. He pulls me closer, onto his lap, pressing our bodies together until there's not even enough room for a bead of sweat to drip between us. My hips rock against him.

I close my eyes, lost in his lips. The world tilts on its axis, spinning fast enough for me to feel the rush but slow enough that I'm not sick. This feeling, this exhilarating, life-changing, lust-falling sensation has nothing to do with the alcohol I've been drinking. It's him and the way my body's reacting to the hardness pressing against my center through his shorts.

He fists my hair, wrapping the sea-sprayed locks that are more knots than loose waves around thick fingers, and pulls my mouth from his. My roots scream, not used to the tingle of pain vibrating through my scalp. But I like it. It pours gasoline on the wave of heat in my belly., making me powerless to the man who thinks I'm something more than what life has let me be.

9

"Do you want to get out of here?"

Yes! A hundred times yes... but I shouldn't. The old version of me liked to play it safe, driving just under the speed limit and checking twice for motorcycles. I never trusted dating sites because of the MTV show Catfish and up until a few months ago I'd never had a one-night stand. I've always been a go slow and feel the guy out kind of girl.

Then, six weeks after Kenny broke my heart, I let loose. I got my first tattoo, drank my heartache away, and found new friends to numb the pain. I realized that, at twenty-one, I was barely living. I existed to make a paycheck and to keep my ex happy.

But I didn't like who I was becoming so I took a break from the sleeping around part. I swore I wouldn't give myself to someone who didn't care about me, and I've been searching for someone who fits that bill for the last two months.

But this is vacation, and I like the way this man's eyes trailing over my body makes me feel. Maybe it's the alcohol, but I doubt I will regret hooking up with this dude when I sober up.

Still, there are some necessities a girl needs to know before riding a new love stick. Like Mcbroody's name, his relationship status, what he does for a living, etcetera. Might as well start with the easy stuff. "Maybe. You got a name?"

"Peter," he breathes, those perfect lips drifting to the side of my neck again.

Peter. I smile, letting myself linger in the moment instead of thinking. I feel Peter's hand slide to my hip and up my back, fingers toying with the strings of my top. I feel his hardness protest against the thin fabric keeping us apart. I feel like I don't care if I'll regret my next move in the morning.

"Wens!" Kierra yells.

I clench my teeth and groan.

Peter's laugh vibrates my skin. He sinks his teeth in my shoulder, pulling a squeal of delight from my lips, then leans back and swallows what's left of his drink. I try to relish the moment and ignore Kierra, but she calls my name again, making it impossible for me to ignore her. It figures she'd be a cock-block.

Just not for my sister because, you know, that would have been helpful.

I force a smile and look her way. Kierra's waving like a maniac to get my attention. "The boat leaves in five!" She gives two thumbs up and waits for me to acknowledge her before walking away.

"Cute nickname." Peter's hand slides down my arm. I shiver as he leans his elbows against the bar. "Is it short for Wendy?"

I don't like the space between us, it makes me anxious. I inch closer until my arm touches his. The thread of tension in my chest thins. He smirks and uses his other hand to sip from his glass.

"No," I say through a laugh.

Although that would have been perfect. Peter and Wendy, like the fairy tale. Destined to have our lives intertwined in adventurous harmony. If starlight wishes came true and book boyfriends were real, I'd be in a magical land with a morally gray prince that gives orgasms just as often as he gives glaring side glances. But my life isn't a story book and I'm not anything special.

"That's a name I could get behind, but no. I drew the short end of the stick."

Peter watches me, waiting for more of an explanation. I don't know why but I feel like I need to tell him the long-standing history of my name. It's an urge, a desperate ache I fear I won't quench if I don't explain.

I don't have a lot of time left, and missing the boat isn't an option. I'm not sure which island we're on or how far we are from the hotel. So, I give Peter the gist of our family's stupidity in one big breath.

"There's a long-standing family tradition of picking a name that starts with a W. Well at least the firstborn girls have a W. It's open season for everyone else. I'm sure there's a Wendy somewhere in the family, but my mom was a hippie without a creative bone in her body and named me Wednesday."

Peter grins a deliciously dark grin that makes me wish I had more time with him. But again... not lucky. He takes my hand and kisses my knuckles. "It was a pleasure to meet you, Wednesday."

"Wens!" Kierra calls again. She taps her wrist and then throws her hands in the air.

I guess my time is up.

"I've got to go." I press a quick kiss to his lips, one I wish was longer, and ended with our clothes on some crappy motel floor.

Fate would throw a beautiful weekend savior in my face only to take him away before any actual saving could be done.

Tyle would lose her mind if I stole her thunder by hooking up with someone before she could. Last night had a strict no dick rule. It was our first night in town, and Tyle wanted to make sure we had at least one whole evening together.

Tonight, however, is fair game and Peter would have been perfect. A distraction from my thoughts. Bragging rights that I hooked up first. A more than decent memory of this trip to look back on. If only time was on my side.

Oh well.

At least I got a kiss out of him. "It was nice to meet you, Peter. Maybe I'll see you around."

"Count on it, Darling."

CHAPTER 3
Wednesday

A tingling sensation down my spine has me peeking over the edge of my eReader, shade from my hat the only thing saving my eyes from the blinding Florida sun.

Somehow the rays seem brighter reflecting off the white concrete and cerulean blue water. Meaner as they shine down on the tropic isles. I don't think I've ever been as tempted to wade into a pool as I am today. Sweat drips down my body in places that have never leaked before in their lives, and it's only mid-morning. I fully understand why everybody runs around half-naked down here. It is literally too hot for clothes.

My eyes take a moment to adjust to the brightness, too used to staring at the darkened screen of my eReader. I wish they hadn't. I should have kept my gaze on the words and not searched for what triggered my spidey sense. I was a lot happier two seconds ago.

"Aou-aou-aou! Sexy mama! Get it, girl!" The bridesmaids I'm forced to spend the weekend with whistle and catcall.

My sister struts down the pool deck, swinging the end of her dress like she's a tigress. Her hair is in a sloppy bun, makeup minimal. She's doing the walk of shame, only today it's a walk of pride.

I shake my head and go back to my book. I don't want to hear about Tyle's sexcapades. Watching her rub how much she loves Kenny in my face every time they're together is hard enough. But hearing how little she respects him makes me angry.

Why take him from me if she was going to cheat?

Why ruin my life just to play with his?

"Sooo? How was it?" Samantha, one of my sister's bridesmaids asks.

"Oh, my gosh, guys." Tyle sits on the edge of Michelle's lounge chair. At least, I think that's her name. I honestly don't remember.

She's got six bridesmaids, and the only person I actually know is Kierra. Everyone else is a friend from work.

People my sister considers to be more important in her life than me.

Tyle pushes long bleached bangs out of her eyes and gives her I've-got-a-story face. "Have you ever given a blowie so bad that while you're doing it you knew it sucked, but the guy didn't say anything so you just kept going?"

I roll my eyes and stare at the paperwhite screen. The words in front of me are a jumbled mess. I try to focus on them, but the longer Tyle talks about her one-night stand the more pissed off I get.

I think the arrangement she made with Kenny is fucked. If you love someone, you shouldn't have a need for strange. When her future husband was mine, I never thought about another man. Hell, I didn't even read romance books because he was all I needed.

Clearly, Kenny didn't feel the same way.

"I knew the moment I started sucking on his crooked thing that everything was wrong." She giggles. "But whatever. I was drunk and it was fun. He got his happy ending—one way or another—and I got some serious man candy to add to my lady spank bank."

A bridesmaid wearing a bright blue bikini and boobs the size of my head hands Tyle a seltzer beer. Apparently, only alcoholics drink liquor before dark and regular beer is for college kids. I don't know who made these rules, but all the girls swear by them. Even Kierra.

I sip on my orange-mango mimosa, inwardly giving every one of them the middle finger, and do my best to tune out their conversation.

Tyle isn't the reason I haven't been able to focus. It's not the book either. Believe me. I can get down with some fae high lords. It's the dude from last night who's got my mind swimming.

Peter.

I haven't felt a fire like the one that shot straight to my lady bits since Kenny kissed me on the Farris wheel my senior year. I thought the lusty haze I felt for tall, dark, and broody was because of the drinks I had, but I'm still thinking about Peter. Still getting a tingle between my legs I don't dare satisfy while sharing a room with seven other girls.

I know it's not likely that I'll see him again. There are seven main keys in Florida, but almost seventeen-hundred little islands. I have no idea where the booze cruise took us yesterday. The pamphlet I saw at the hotel said we started in Key Largo, but we went to six other bars, all of which claimed to be secret hot spots, plus drank on the way to each location. For all I know we were taken to some private resort bar only accessible by boats. The chances of Peter's and my path crossing again are slim, but damn I hope they do.

"What!" My sister squeals, pulling me out of my thoughts. "Wednesday! You found a man last night?"

Tyle shimmies and shakes, I think trying to make a sexy gesture with her body. If that's the coordination her boy-toy got last night, it's no wonder the man didn't say anything about the BJ. If she were to try harder the poor dude probably would have thought he stuck his dick in a meat grinder.

"I want all the dirty details, you little whore." Tyle scoots to my lounge chair and wiggles herself beside me.

Five years ago I would have shifted onto my side and cuddled up next to her. The guys at school loved to see us close... fucking pervs. But we're not sixteen anymore. We're twenty-one and I have a hard time even looking at my sister these days, let alone giving her snuggles.

I pull my legs in close then turn sideways to sit on the chair's edge. I doubt Tyle notices the inch of air between us. She hasn't noticed the wedge she created the summer we turned fifteen growing wider with each passing year. Why would she notice an extra inch?

"Not sure what to say. I can't remember very much. That last bartender was amazing."

"Oh, em, gee. She made me something called a Purple Hooter Shooter." Tyle looks at the girls and raises her eyebrows. "Y'all... best thing I put in my mouth all night."

I force a smile at her joke while bile climbs my throat. How is she okay with this? How is she okay with Kenny doing the same thing? Pressing his lips against some other chick's neck. Touching her like he cares. Taking all of their intimate moments and sharing the tricks that are solely hers with someone else.

I shudder, unable to take it anymore. I'm used to my mind straying to Kenny's sex life, especially at the beginning of their relationship. Wondering how many of the moves I taught him he's used on my sister.

It still makes me sick.

But this is somehow worse because a small twisted part of me hoped Kenny would use this pass to give us one more chance. Our last bedroom romp was horrible. He was frustrated because he couldn't get it up and I was a mess thinking I was the problem.

Turns out the problem was that I wasn't Tyle.

I may be crazy, looking into the sideways glances Kenny sends my way, or the extra second eye locks, but... I don't know. I thought he wanted to give us closure.

I would have ditched Tyle's bachelorette party in a heartbeat to show up at Kenny's door. For one, he used to be a great lay. I would have climbed onto his cock and rode him until he was at the brink of coming and then walked away. That man deserves a serious case of blue balls after how he screwed me over.

But the bragging rights that Kenny still wanted me would have been the ultimate slap in the face to Tyle.

I smile inwardly, thinking about the conversation we would have had after the fact, but of course, things didn't pan out that way. Instead, Kenny is sharing what used to be our intimate tricks with someone new. Once again throwing it in my face that I'm not good enough.

I skip the straw in my glass and take the rest of my drink like a shot. I can feel judgy eyes on me as I gulp half of a champagne flute in one swallow, but truthfully I couldn't care less about what these bitches think.

Fun fact about Tyle and me... we're different. Besides the ugly truth that I'm not a heartless whore, who's paid to look like a blonde Kardashian, I have no gag reflex.

We both know that she'd choke the moment her mouth got full. That's why she mumbles *drunk* under her breath as I swallow. She knows that no matter how hard she tries, I will always suck dick better than her.

Am I proud of that?

Eh... it's not something I flaunt, but today it feels good.

I moan and wipe my mouth, channeling my inner porn star just for the sake of adding more awkwardness. I'm ninety-percent sure Tyle's oral exam last night was meant to be practice for the wedding night.

Kenny loved to try and choke me with his monster—and believe me it's a monster—but I never gagged. Better get practicing, bitch.

"I'm heading up to the room." I don't give anyone a chance to respond. The chair tips when I stand. Tyle squeals like the helpless little bird she is and falls to the floor. Her friends scramble to help her back onto her feet, fussing over superficial scrapes and dirt.

As for me... I steal Tyle's seltzer beer and take it with me. I may not be a fan of this shit, but she took what was mine.

It's only fair I return the favor.

CHAPTER 4
Wednesday

I think my sister's sole purpose in life is to torment me.

She knows I hate the ocean.

Not the beach. I like the feel of sand and tiny shells between my toes. I like sitting on the shore as waves cool my sun-kissed skin. I love relaxing with a book and a bucket of something tasty while birds fly across the sky. I even enjoy laying on a foam board and riding baby waves onto the skinny water while gliding across the sand.

And I can get behind watching man candy play volleyball or football, or even frisbee so long as it requires him to have his shirt off.

What I don't like is being in water that's more than waist-deep.

Which is why I hate the glass-bottom-boat tour she's scheduled for today. Its sole purpose in life is to prove just how much more than waist-deep the ocean is. We haven't passed over any coral or a noticeable seafloor. I haven't seen a fish, a dolphin... nothing. There's just a never ending swipe of blue on a much too big canvas both above and below the water.

Even if the bottom wasn't plexiglass and I couldn't see beyond the hull, I would still hate this boat. The double-decker, hundred and twenty foot, vessel is fully air-conditioned, staffed with a captain, three servers, as well as a swim crew. It is the Titanic of glass-bottom tours, minus the sinking.

But even if this boat was the infamously sinkable cruise ship, where I was guaranteed a hot hookup, a lifeboat, and a multi-million dollar diamond at the end of our voyage I would still despise it, just like I despised yesterday's sportfish.

Because I can't swim.

My worst fear is falling into the water and drowning. It's so bad I can barely go by a pool. I'm terrified someone will throw me in, thinking the prank is harmless, and I'll inhale too much water and then die.

My logic may be dramatic, but I have my reasons. I never used to be like this. When we were little, I loved being in the water. I still love it. If we're going someplace with a pool I usually find a chair at the shallowest end and stay next to the steps, dipping my toes in.

On the rare occasion I venture deeper, I stay on my feet. I don't like floats or rafts because they can drift to the deep end and I won't go in if the water is the slightest bit cold. Shivering half-naked isn't my idea of fun. Most of my friends know about my fear of water and they're respectful.

But I'll never forget the summer Tyle dared her boyfriend to throw me into the community pool. He tossed me in the shallows, but at the time I didn't know.

All I saw was light filtering through from above.

All I felt was the suffocating pressure pushing my body deeper and deeper until my skin scraped against the cement floor.

I was underwater for less than ten seconds, but every tick of the second hand felt like hours. Kenny immediately jumped in and pulled me to the surface. I clung to him, desperately trying not to cry while our friends laughed.

I wasn't in any real danger, they said. The prank was harmless but to me, I felt like I had been violated. I didn't talk to my sister for the rest of the summer, and I think that's the moment I started pushing our circle away. I couldn't trust any of them.

My hand shakes just thinking about that day and how easy it would be for something similar to happen again. At least there's a bar on board the boat to alleviate some of my anxiety, and two stories to lounge on. Although, for some reason, being on the top deck makes me queasy. Maybe it's being able to see all the water around me, a stretch of deep blue that haunts my thoughts like a never-ending nightmare.

"Thanks." I stuff a five-dollar bill into the tip jar and immediately bring the rim of my glass to my lips. I close my eyes as I take the first sip of what will probably be many glasses. My concoction, liquid marijuana, is cold and bitter with the right amount of sweetness.

"You make the most delicious sounds."

I choke on my green drink. The little hairs on my arms stand on edge. My body is angry at my sudden stupidity of confusing a cocktail for air, yet excited because I recognize the voice.

Peter wipes a calloused thumb across my chin, erasing tiny green droplets that missed my mouth. I wonder what he does for a living to have such textured hands, or if the roughness is from lifting weights. He's got the body to show for that kind of hard work. All sharp edges and smooth lines.

Peter's lips lift in a smile that demands to be kissed. God, he's pretty. I still haven't figured out how someone as beautiful as him is single. Or maybe he's not. Maybe he's married and a shitty husband or in an open relationship. I know nothing about him and I really don't want to ask.

Does that make me a bad person? Probably, but as long as I don't do anything crazy my conscience will survive.

I lean in for a hug as the boat rolls over a large wave. It throws me off balance. I stumble backward, spilling half my drink onto the bartender's table.

Peter wraps his arms around my waist and pulls me close, steadying me on my feet. "Easy, Darling. It would be a shame to lose you so soon."

My arm goes around his neck on instinct. Being this close again is dangerous. Yesterday's desire paired with today's anxiety is a lethal combination. I hope no one needs the bathroom for a while because if things go my way, we'll be occupying it for a long time.

We lock eyes, his gaze devouring me in a way I wish his lips would. Heat climbs my cheeks and I'm smiling again, feeling like a kid with her first crush all over again. "Thanks."

Peter smells just like I remember. Rich, with a hint of earth, sage, and bad decisions. The scent penetrates my senses, making each one itch to be satisfied.

His fingers play with the strings of my forest green bikini top at my back. I stole this one from Tyle's suitcase because it reminded me of Peter. Not this Peter but the one from the story about Neverland, and in a roundabout way it made me feel close to this Peter.

It made sense at the time, but now as I think about the choice again, it sounds crazy. I look into this Peter's eyes, falling deeper into their abyss. Like the ocean, their deep-set blue makes me quiver, but for a more enjoyable reason.

Peter's grin shifts into a goofy one, wide, two dimples on display. For a moment, I can see it. Him being some grown-up version of the boy who refused to age, hardened by life but still playful at heart. I imagine him flying and crowing and causing chaos only to find his way into my bed once the sun went down because, let's be real, fantasizing about a kid is weird, but thinking of a grown man who left his fictional girlfriend for me... way better.

I push the ludicracy away and make a mental note to find some kind of Peter Pan retelling when I have cell service again to download to the eReader app. "What are you doing here?"

Peter doesn't let me go, even as my hand slides down his bare chest, feeling the baby hairs that cover those dark tattoos. I trace a line with my finger, following it from his collar bone to his sternum. His muscles are hard. Warm. The line keeps going, intertwining with more than a dozen others, creating new paths on his body. I'm lost in the gorgeousness that is him...until his deep whisper brings me back to reality.

"I wanted to see the beauties beneath the sea." His voice sends a shudder of delight through me. I can't explain it, the warm, needy sensation that trails through my veins like liquid gold.

But I like it.

"Although, I'm not complaining about what I found above it." His finger traces a small circle on my lower back. "What about you, Wednesday? What are you doing on this boat?"

"Oh, you know. Fulfilling my mission to help my sister check every box on her bachelorette bucket list." I roll my eyes because this particular ocean tour ends with optional snorkeling and she has every intention of losing her top in the water. The only reason I agreed to come is because it is an adult cruise. The last thing we need is a pissed off parent because her pepperoni nipples scarred some kid for life.

I hear Tyle's voice carry across the room. I can recognize her anywhere, and it's not even a twin thing. Tyle just has that voice. High-pitched, notoriously upbeat, and all around fake.

"Worst idea ever," my sister declares, talking to her bridesmaids. She struts across the teak, her heels click click clicking as she sways her hips. Every step is exaggerated, meant to draw the eyes of anyone who will look. Tyle doesn't care if it's male, female, or gender-neutral so long as people are paying attention to her.

She frowns when she sees me, her eyebrows drawing into a straight line. She signals her pose to hang back. And they do, staring and whispering amongst themselves with sinister grins as Tyle walks toward us.

I look Peter in his royal blue eyes, knowing the game that's about to begin, and see all possibilities of what could have been fade away. The moment his gaze settles on her, I feel it in my soul.

It's game over for me.

CHAPTER 5
Wednesday

y stomach twists into a dozen knots. Nerves, disappointment, alcohol, and the rocking of the boat merge together and morph into nausea. I fight the bile climbing my throat. Throwing up everywhere would give me an escape from what I'm about to witness, but I don't want to leave.

There's an invisible string between Peter and me, pulling tighter, drawing us closer with every minute we're together. If I believed in love at first sight, I'd tell the world that's what this is because my body craves his touch as much as my ears beg to listen to his voice. A small part of me has hope that this unexplainable bond between us is enough to evade Tyle's thirst trap.

Still, I can't stand the thought of Peter touching me if he falls under my sister's spell. It hits too close to home. The pain from my last relationship is too fresh, the bandaid covering my scars ripped off by what's about to go down.

I move my hand from the waistband of Peter's bathing suit, my fingers having just found the curls at the end of his happy trail, and step backward.

Peter's grip loosens, but he still holds my waist. His hands burn my hips, heat from my anxiety and neediness mix together. I arch my back, putting as much distance between us as I can. He lets me go with a frown.

Tyle flashes her signature smile, showcasing perfectly white veneers as she comes closer. I'm sure she assumes she's already won. My pulling away the white flag. I'm not going to fight over a man, no matter how much I like him, and she knows it.

Tyle glides the tips of her manicured nails down the curves of Peter's arm. The same feeling I get when she kisses Kenny blooms in my chest. A tightness that spreads from my sternum to my back. It squeezes the air from my lungs, shooting needles down my spine.

I hate this.

Watching her take what could have been mine.

Again.

Kierra asked me once, back when we were in high school, why I allowed Tyle to walk all over me. She assumed I let my sister flirt with the boys I liked and willingly turned my back when she made them hers under the bleachers.

The truth was that every time my sister manipulated a man into choosing her over me, another crack set in. Another voice of doubt and discouragement whispered in my mind until there was no point in trying anymore.

It didn't matter if Tyle had a boyfriend or not. She couldn't stand the thought of a guy looking at me and so she made him only have eyes for her. She lived for the attention and then discarded him once she had it.

Today is no different.

I could easily lean into Peter and hope this energy bouncing between us is enough to dissuade her charms, but I don't want a man who would choose my sister over me. I want someone who ignores Tyle's pretty face and sees her for the snake she is.

If Peter falls into her thirst trap, I'm better off without him. Even if a small part of me already hurts at the thought of letting him go.

"O.M.G. Your tattoo is fabulous," my sister purrs.

I watch Peter, mentally preparing for the grin that has sent butterflies a flight within me to flash for Tyle. The only man I knew who could resist her seductive green eyes and ruby red lips gave into temptation. It took years, but she got her way.

I don't have high hopes today.

Tyle is sex in heels, whereas I'm a bookworm with some extra love on my hips and hair that's lucky to see a blowdryer on the weekend. She's the kind of woman men fantasize about. While I'm the girl they leave their kids with and not think twice about it before walking out the door.

Peter's blue eyes darken and shift in color. Black spills into them like ink in water until there isn't any azure left. He clenches his jaw, showing one tick of frustration, and then it's gone, wiped away as if it never existed.

The bartender at the counter behind us hands Peter a glass of amber liquor. I don't remember him ordering, but he must have, probably when I was lost in the patterns of his tattoo. He brings his lips to the glass and takes a sip without so much as sparing a passing glance at my sister.

Tyle forces her grin wider. Men don't usually respond to her this way. She's used to them chasing her like love drunk fools. Peter is impassive, barely acknowledging her existence. If I know my sister like I think I do, it's eating her alive.

Tyle presses her chest against Peter's arm. Her pretty white-tipped nails run down the length of his spine. Her fingers stretch wide, touching the muscles of his bare back.

I turn away from them and ask the bartender for a cup of water. I don't feel so good again and I don't think drowning my thoughts in alcohol is a good idea. Not when Tyle can see I'm bothered.

I refuse to give her the satisfaction.

"Is that a picture of Neverland?" Tyle asks, her voice a whisper of seduction. "*Peter and Wendy* is my favorite Disney retelling."

Liar. It's mine and she knows it. I force the huff of breath to ease out my nostrils, slow and controlled. It's just one more thing to add to the list of items Tyle took from me.

"Don't touch me," Peter growls, jerking his arm away.

The sheer hatred in his tone makes me jump. I should be scared or at least put-off. Logically, I know a man who reacts to a woman with such harshness is dangerous. I shouldn't feel the tingle of lust between my legs, but dear god it's hot watching him reject my sister.

Tyle holds her hands up and mock-surrenders and steps to where he can see her pouty face. "Sorry, pumpkin. I didn't realize you had a kink."

"Peter, this is my sister Tyle." The introduction is like ash in my mouth. I know it's what she's been waiting for. After all, in her eyes, married or not, I will forever be her wing-woman. The only reason I'm even bothering is because I'm curious as to what Peter will do next.

"Oh, my God. Your name is Peter?" Tyle squeals and touches his arm again. Peter's gaze narrows on her hand. He frowns, but Tyle is oblivious to his discomfort. "I have some role play fantasies that I'm dying to try, if you're into that kind of thing."

Peter grips his glass until his knuckles flash white, somehow managing to keep his features indifferent. He lifts his tumbler of whiskey, ice clinking along the sides, but pauses before drinking and says, "Sweetheart, you couldn't handle me in bed."

He takes a sip of the whiskey, his gaze trailing from Tyle to me, and then grins. "But I have a feeling this one here knows how to have a good time."

"Wednesday?" My sister scoffs. Her eyes roll so hard I'm surprised they're still in her head. "Please, she's so vanilla. Her boyfriend dumped her six months ago because he got bored screwing her. Poor thing hasn't had a man in her life since." She touches my arm, pho-sympathy on her face. "Bless your heart, darlin'."

The nagging burn of tears pricks my eyes. Tyle knows how to hit me where it hurts. She knows her betrayal is a barely closed wound on my heart, one she likes to poke and reopen any chance she can.

I force the knot of hurt in my throat down and try to smile. If I do anything else, even something as deserved as defending myself, the dam will break free and I'll be a blubbering mess. That's what she wants though. Isn't it? To destroy what little chance I might have with Peter by any means necessary.

I almost wonder if Tyle is even attracted to him—Peter doesn't fit our usual go-to man—or if she just wants his attention because he's talking to me.

I know I said I don't want a guy who would leave me for her, and I stand by that, but I don't understand why she can't just respect what's mine.

Why does she always have to take, and take, and take?

It's not enough for her to marry the only man I've ever loved. She has to screw my rebound too.

Peter doesn't miss a beat. He looks me in the eye again. That dark matter I can't explain swirls in the blue of his irises. I've never seen anything like it. It's fascinating, so much so that I almost miss his response. "Vanilla is my favorite flavor."

My jaw drops at the same time Tyle's nearly hits the floor.

"Come on, Darling." Peter reached for my hand and threads our fingers together. His touch is colder than I remember, but the tingle of nervous energy in my palm offsets the chill. "You and I have some unfinished business to attend to."

"Oh, my God!" Tyle squeals, her voice reaching an octave only dogs should hear. "You're him! You're the guy from the bar last night." She turns her attention to me, a disappointed frown tilting her lips. "Jesus, Wednesday. How could you forget a hunk like that?" Her eyes drag back to Peter with an *I'm so sorry* look. "Yeah, she forgot all about you. Couldn't tell us a single thing, not even your name."

"I promise you, Cabinet, your sister did not forget about me." Peter's thumb rubs circles against my skin. His touch steady. Soothing. "If I was a betting man, I'd say Wednesday was trying to save me from the likes of you, but what she doesn't realize is that I've dealt with monsters that have slimier tentacles than yours." He pauses, smirking to himself. "Although, I will say, you give those beasts a run for their money."

"My name is Tyle," she mutters through clenched teeth.

"And I don't care." Peter releases my fingers to wrap his arm around my waist. I lean into him, my heart racing, my mind replaying the last five minutes. I've never seen a man blatantly reject Tyle before.

And he did it for me.

CHAPTER 6
Wednesday

Peter and I walk to the stern of the boat. There's only one couple back here with us. A man in a button-down shirt with hula-girls on it and a woman with a big purple hat that shadows most of her face. The woman leans into the man, touching his arm when they talk. Pressing her body close.

"Do you think they came together or are having some boat-loving fun?" I wonder out loud. I watch the couple, curious about what outsiders see when they look at Peter and me. We look about as matched as Oreos and whiskey. Separate each one is amazing but together...not so much.

Peter stares off at the horizon. His brows are pulled close together, his thoughts far from where we stand.

"Peter?"

"Hmmm?"

"You're not having buyer's remorse. Are you?" Something falls into the pit of my stomach. A knot, or maybe my heart. Hard to say at this point, but it leaves me feeling hollow.

Maybe I jumped to conclusions thinking he was better than the rest.

Maybe he likes to argue and that show of power was foreplay.

Maybe I read our situation all wrong.

That last thought makes me sad. I hope not. Peter makes me feel good and worthy of attention. Forever being in my sister's shadow has messed with my confidence. It got better when Kenny was around, but the floor fell out from under me with that one. I hate the doubt I'm feeling, but better to find out now that I'm being used than three years from now and have my heart incinerated again.

"If you want to go back to Tyle, you can. She won't care." I force myself to laugh because I feel like I'm crumbling. "Hell, it'll probably turn her on if you reject me now."

"Darling." Peter threads his fingers through the hair at the base of my neck and pulls me close until our chests are pressing against each other. He looks me in the eyes with unwavering confidence. Inky darkness spills into the deep blue of his irises. "There are a million women in existence throughout the universe, but there is no other soul in all the galaxies like yours. I would choose you over her every day, with every breath."

Heat flushes my face and chest. I bite my lip, convinced my face is beat red. No one has ever said something so beautiful to me. My knees buckle and I reach for the deck railing with one hand to steady myself. I feel like I'm standing naked for all the world to see, all of my insecurities exposed because for the first time in months I feel something more than hazy lust and anger.

I feel vulnerable.

It's crazy that a man I met only yesterday has such control over my emotions. It doesn't make sense, but the terror that Peter will walk away and never see me again is as real as the sweat dripping down my back. It's unwelcome and inconvenient and messy, but it's there.

"So...what's wrong?" I whisper.

"I'm trying to decide what to do with you." He pauses. His fingers pull at my roots again, inching our faces closer together. I stare into his eyes. That beautiful blue swallows the black ink that danced within his irises. They're normal again, a blue ring surrounding onyx pupils. How do they do that?

Peter's fingers unfurl from my roots. He turns and sits against the edge of the boat. "Play a game with me, Darling."

"All right." I mimic his pose. My heart beats faster, doubling in speed with each thump. I take a deep breath and convince myself I'm okay. We're slow-cruising. Taking our time so everyone aboard can enjoy the scenery. The seas are calm-ish, clear. The chances of me falling overboard are one in a million and even if I did, I'm fairly confident Peter would save me.

I. Will. Be. Fine.

"Truth or dare." There's a glimmer of mischievousness in the way he asks. The kind expected from a teenage boy, just before they do something stupid. Peter is a far cry from a teenager. If I had to guess, I'd say he's in his mid-twenties and no part that I can see is boy.

"Truth." Dares are dangerous. He could tell me to disappear with him and I would, in a heartbeat, because my soul feels like it's splitting in two. There's an ache resonating in my bones that's only quenched when his hands are on my body. Maybe I should have said dare.

"Okay. Ask away."

I laugh, confused by his response. "That's not how the game works. You're supposed to ask me a question."

Peter drags his teeth across his bottom lip. The movement is slow. Deliberate. Meant to make me look at his mouth and I do. I remember the way his lips felt against mine, how his tongue moved expertly. I imagine it's as skilled on other parts of the body. I press my thighs together, embarrassed by the wetness pooling in my panties.

"Scared of the answers, Darling?" He eases closer, dropping his voice to a gruff sexy low. "I know there's something looming in your mind. I can see it on your lips."

"Am I that obvious?" I tuck wayward strands that have wiggled loose from my braid behind my ears. They tickle my nose and cheeks, blowing in the breeze. The feeling isn't uncomfortable, but the fact that Peter can so clearly see through my guard is.

"You possess the beautiful ability to display how you feel without using words. All I needed to do is look at you to see that your little mind is running in circles. Ask me what you want to know, Darling." He touches my chin. The rough pad of his thumb brushes over my bottom lip. "I'll only ever tell you the truth."

My cheeks heat again, proving his point that I can't hide how I'm feeling. Peter chuckles at my embarrassment. I let out a slow breath, then meet his gaze again. I need to look him in the eye for this. "Do you have a wife? Or girlfriend? Or someone who would be upset at what we're doing?"

He tilts his head, thinking. "I am neither formally nor informally committed to anyone, but I'm sure there are plenty who would be unhappy that you have my undivided attention."

Neither a lie nor a truth. The sneaky bastard kept his word.

"Your turn." Peter takes my hand in his and flips it over. He traces

30

the lines on my palm with the edge of his nail. Pressing hard enough that the sensation tickles, but doesn't hurt. "Favorite color?"

"Really?" Such a loaded question. My favorite color changes with my mood. I can never pick just one. Even as a child I would ramble off four or five at a time, never the same ones in a row. "I don't know. Green, I guess. What about you?"

"Blue, like that of the sky." He glances upwards, a playful grin on his face but there's a shadow of sadness that looks out of place. "My turn. What is your greatest fear?"

"Wow. Going deep. Um... drowning. I can't swim."

"And you're on a boat?"

"Never claimed to be the sharpest crayon in the box."

"Well, Darling, I was going to ask if you were daring, but I think I have my answer." He smirks again. I don't think I've ever seen a man as happy as him. It's like the weight of life doesn't fall on his shoulders. My job, all the bills I have to pay, and the decisions I've made in the past make it hard to enjoy life. But Peter... he's pure joy wrapped in tattoos and muscles. "You're the bravest girl on the boat."

"I wouldn't go that far. More like stupidly eager to please."

Peter's hand covers mine. He turns my wrist over and kisses my knuckles. His lips are pillow soft against my skin and send a surge of excitement all the way down to my toes. "I want the biggest truth of them all, Darling. Whatever the answer, you cannot lie. Promise me."

"I promise," I say, anticipation sucking the breath from my lungs.

"Would you come away with me, Wednesday? Leave your sister's pettiness behind and have the adventure of a lifetime." He squeezes my hand in his, holding onto me with so much hope it radiates off him in waves of yellow and gold. "There is so much I can show you, so much we can do together. You'll never have to worry about anything again. What do you say?"

I laugh, unsure of how to respond. This is crazy. No sane woman runs away with a man she just met, even if he is panty-dropping hot. This is how women go missing and end up trafficked. I can't leave. I won't leave.

But this is just a game.

I can pretend for a few minutes that Peter is everything he seems to be and more. For all I know, he's a wealthy businessman ready to whisk me away on a private jet to some tropical island. That would be nice. I toy with my thoughts, imagining what it would be like to disappear and live extravagantly without worrying about money or my sister or any part of day-to-day life.

Tonight, I'll go back to my hotel and we'll all go out one more time before heading home tomorrow. Maybe I'll see Peter again before I leave. Maybe I won't. Either way, what harm can come from playing a game and giving the answer I wish could be true?

"Yes."

Peter grins. "I was hoping you'd say that."

He presses his lips to mine but they pull away far too quickly. "You're perfect, Darling. Absolutely perfect."

Without warning, Peter pushes my shoulder. I fall backward, over the ledge of the boat. The cold Florida water hits my skin and sucks the air from my lungs before I can scream. My arms flail, and my legs kick, but they don't work together. A shadow passes over the sun's rays as they permeate through the water.

Someone will come for me.

I'll be okay.

A burning ache spreads in my lungs with each second that ticks by and I realize I'm alone.

My organs are desperate for air, and the longer I'm without the harder it is to make my body cooperate. My limbs get heavier. Harder to move. But I push through the pain.

Today is not my day to die.

I will fight until my heart quits because as hard as my life is, as much suffering as it's caused me, I'm not ready to give it up. There's too much I haven't done. I want to get married and have kids and travel the world. I want to find the little moments and live within them. This can't be the end.

I don't know how much time passes, but a breath of ice coats my skin.

And then it all goes dark.

CHAPTER 7
Peter

I kick the edge of the doorstep before crossing inside, knocking the dirt off my boots. It's been decades since I stepped into the realm of the living. I forgot how long the journey from the mirror pool to the tree house is and how taxing it is to go from The Triangle to Neverland.

I'm tired.

Too tired to clean up a muddy mess.

Wednesday has yet to wake, the journey more strenuous on her than me. She turns in my arms and hugs close to my chest. Her mouth falls open and drool drips down her cheek, pooling against my skin. I force my mouth to hold steady and fight a grin. The war against my emotions begins now. Before she realizes what I've done or who she is.

Casper Greenbrier, my right-hand man, sits in the faded wingback chair by the window, a tattered novel in his hands. Waiting for me. "Taking a page out of your brother's book, Peter?"

I shake my head, ignoring the dig. I'm nothing like James. Not anymore. "This one is different. It's her."

"How do you know?"

I look at my shadow. The part of my soul I sacrificed to save the only person I've ever loved. The devils I bargained with gave him free will and the ability to leave my side, taking my gift of flight with him. A cruel corollary to the promise made, but that's what the fae do. They twist the truth until there are so many turns it could be a lie.

Back then, if I knew the true price of saving Wendy Darling's life, I would have found another way.

My shadow self leaves the comforts of the counter he perches on. He walks to me along the wall, taking his time, knowing Cass is judging his every step.

The funny thing about my shadow, he may be his own being, but our thoughts are connected. I can feel his excitement and fears despite being inches away or halfway across the world, and he can read my mind. Whether or not he listens is another story.

Today he seems amicable. My shadow slides along the floor to place his feet on top of mine and climbs into my skin. He slithers, getting comfortable. Even though he's made himself home inside me again the past two days, it's jarring having him there. Two minds. One body. Forever at war with each other.

The power I lost bleeds out of Shadow and into my veins, igniting like sparklers in my blood. On Earth, the sensation was an annoying tingle, painfully waiting to be awoken. Here, I'm connected to the Island again. We're one, like we were so long ago.

It feels good.

I let out a controlled breath and school my features into passiveness. The only tell that his power, my power, flows through me again is the onyx in my eyes. Shadow's presence fills them, masking my blues with his darkness. I didn't realize he could do that until I saw my reflection yesterday. He and I haven't been together since that fateful day.

"Holy shit," Cass mumbles. He sets the leather bound book on my end table and stands. "It is her."

I nod, the gravity of Wednesday's presence falling harder against me. Cass's kin created the curse I live with. He and his siblings, Belle and Emmit, are the only fae on the island, but none of them were there that night. They don't know everything I sacrificed or what her soul's return means for all of us.

Cass has an idea. He's the only person who understands what I've done. What I've condemned us all to. I see the moment he realizes what having Wednesday in Neverland could mean for The Lost. "How did you get the Darling here?"

"By doing something she'll never forgive me for."

Cass rubs the back of his neck and sighs. There are two paths into Neverland: through the sky or a portal. Neither of which can be navigated with a fully beating heart. I carry the guilt of every soul that crosses into this realm. Most were brought by James or happenstance, but it's because of what I did that they are eternal prisoners of the island.

"Sounds about right." Cass stares at Wednesday's chest, watching the rise and fall of her lungs with each breath. His brows draw together as the dots connect before him. "She's still alive? How?"

"A little bit of luck mixed with a lot of magic." I lift my chin toward Wendy Darling's old room. I haven't been there in ages. The sheets are probably dust-covered, along with the rest of her furniture. All of Wendy's personal items are with James. I have nothing left of her but haunting memories and an empty space. "Think she'd like that one? Or should I give her my room?"

"No. That one should be good. With any luck, it'll trigger a forgotten memory and make the transition easier." Cass walks to the kitchen, if it could be called that. The tree houses don't have modern amenities. Appliances like a fridge or stove are useless without gas or electricity, but I have cabinets with cups and plates and a drawer of silverware. Cass doesn't reach for those. Instead, he grabs a bucket from under the counter, a clean set of sheets, and a wash rag. "Sit with her. You've had a long night. I'll get the room ready."

I take a seat in the chair by the window, setting the majority of Wednesday's weight on my lap. The poor girl is still out cold, her breaths a slow steady intake as she sleeps. I watch her while Cass cleans, reliving our last moments together in my mind.

The terror of witnessing Wednesday die and the regret of using her weakness against her hangs on me. I don't miss this part of my shadow.

The feelings.

Shadow took those with him a long time ago and I was comfortably numb, free of ailments like pain or sorrow. Until his excitement hit me like a sledgehammer to the face the other day. He called to me, begging me to join him in the human world.

And so I did.

I think the fear he holds is the most jarring. I feel it like it's my own. Strong. All consuming.

If my shadow found Wednesday, that means James could have too, and that makes Shadow's bones shake.

After all these years, James never stopped searching for Wendy's reincarnation. Girls, boys, dogs... if he thought there was a chance our Darling had returned, he took them. Killed them in hopes they'd survive the journey and disposed of the bodies when they didn't. It physically hurts me to think about what could happen if he discovers Wednesday.

"It's ready."

I meet Cass's gaze. He gives me a sad smile. We both know Wednesday can't stay. It's too dangerous, but we have to find a way to keep her safe. At least if she's with us we know she isn't with him.

"She'll never trust me." The admission is a knife to the chest. People like me don't get second chances. Not after what I've done. But Wednesday's beating heart is the missing piece. The antidote to our curse. Our second chance if I can figure out how to break the curse without permanently taking her life.

I stand, careful not to drop Wednesday in the process. She's pitifully light, but I'm drained. It's been so long since I've wielded magic. I forgot how taxing it is.

"She might. It just depends on how she wakes."

Meaning which emotion is prevalent. Neverland holds the soul in their last moment of life. I'm hoping that Wednesday's beating heart didn't trap her in an eternal state of fear. It's taken Scarlett—one of our Lost souls—decades to manage her terror.

Wednesday doesn't have that kind of time.

"I need you to be her hero, Cass." A knot lodges itself in my chest, but I know this is for the best. Wednesday needs to trust someone on the Island. She needs an ally. I can't be that person for her. "No matter the cost, keep her safe from everyone. In her eyes, I'm the bad guy. Let me be her villain. If she hates me, it will make my next move bearable."

I lay Wednesday on the bed and touch her cheek one last time. I doubt she'll let me get this close again. Probably for the best. I've already let myself fall too far down an old path.

"Peter."

"Tell the others to play along, Cass." I pull the thin sheet he found over her shoulders. Water bleeds onto the fabric from her bathing suit. Green under white. The colors of life and death. "I'll set the plan in motion when she wakes. After that, she's all yours."

Cass frowns. He believes there's another way, but he's wrong. My soulmate gave her heart to my brother, and I gave away my soul. There was always a chance the Gods would allow her to live again, but the fae made sure we could never be together.

If Wednesday's heart is claimed before James can find her, the curse will be broken.

I think.

I hope.

CHAPTER 8
Wednesday

I suck in a sharp breath, jolting myself awake. All I see around me is darkness, a black hole void of light or shadows. I remember the darkness as it pulled me beneath the water. The way its cold hands wrapped around my neck, pushing me deeper into its trenches. No matter how hard I clawed, I couldn't reach the surface. My lungs burned, desperate for air. My chest felt like it was being torn apart.

I touch my chest, desperate to feel my own heartbeat. Its consistent thump, thump, thumps makes me sigh a breath of relief.

I survived.

Somehow, someone must have pulled me out of the water. Gave me CPR, and brought me...here. Wherever here is.

The flame of a lighter flickers in the room. I sit up. Someone's thumb rakes against the wheel. Light. No light. Light. No light. Until finally the flame holds steady, pressed to the wick of a candle or something similar.

Shadows reach out from the darkness that covers us like a blanket. Another candle is lit, this one at the base of the wall on the far end of the room. Yellow light stretches up, touching the bare wood, kissing the hue of the beam strewn beside it.

One by one, the perimeter illuminates. I follow the path with my gaze, taking in each shadowed item in the room. There's a dresser on one end. A small desk and chair are on the wall across from it. I'm in a bed, this much I can tell. The mattress beneath me is soft, the blankets light.

I curl my legs in, folding them to sit crossed. Each new light is a piece of the puzzle. It's terrifying, not knowing what's coming next, but exciting too. Like unwrapping a present at Christmas.

The next candle lights beside the bed. I scream, finding dark eyes staring into mine, and swing on instinct. A hand curls around my fist, tingles spreading from the touch of his skin down my core.

It's then I realize who's eyes I'm looking at. I recognize them as I would my own in a mirror.

Peter sits in a chair, arms crossed over the wooden frame where his back should rest. There's something different about him. A coldness I didn't notice on the boat or the bar.

"I was wondering when you'd wake," he says and even his voice has an edge to it that I don't recall. "I hoped you'd still have that fire in you. Death is unpredictable. Sometimes people come back... different."

Flashes of memories come back to me in broken pieces. My skin heats as it remembers the way Peter's hands felt on me. My neck tingles in the place his lips caressed. I reach up and touch that spot, a small smile lifting my lips. But then I remember his palm on my chest and the cold rush of water that came after.

"You pushed me." I don't realize I said the words out loud until Peter nods once, his eyes chained to me.

"Dying is the greatest adventure of them all." He says it in such a childlike way, filled with wonder and unhindered belief, I can't help but laugh once.

"I don't want to die, Peter." My voice cracks when I say his name, revealing how vulnerable I am. I hate that my insecurity is out there for him to see. I'm not this person. I don't cry in public, I don't get mad and blow my top. I'm the calm twin. The one everyone turns to when shit hits the fan. I keep the world together when everything falls apart. But I'm cracking. "I didn't want any of this."

"Liar!" Peter stands and throws the chair in one swift movement. It shatters into a dozen pieces across the room. I flinch out of reflex and he snarls.

"Take me home, Peter." I cross my arms. "Or so help the stars in the sky, I will make you regret bringing me here." I narrow my eyes and glare, hoping the paper-thin armor I'm wearing doesn't fall apart. I don't know how I'll make him regret bringing me here—wherever here is—but I will find a way.

Peter frowns but nods, visibly at war with himself. His expression softens and he sighs. "I'm sorry, Darling."

I drop my arms and try not to cling to the hope that I've won the argument. The cynic in me says that was too easy, but the terrified, pissed-off woman in me is squeezing that shred of hope to the point of suffocation.

Peter drops his head back. He looks at the ceiling, staring with such determination, searching for something far off in the distance, beyond the walls that cage us.

"All is not lost," he says after a long pause. Those dark blues, nearly black with whatever swirls inside them, find mine. "There's still time."

"Time for what?"

He smirks. A devilish grin devours the sweet, boyish innocence he radiated. "Tick. Tock. Tick. Tock. Never fear time on a broken clock. Don't worry, Darling. While you're here we'll be sure you have fun."

"I don't want to have fun, Peter. I want to go home!" He can't do this. He can't keep me here. In this room. On this island.

Peter ignores me. He chants the same, confusing rhyme as he leaves me on the bed. The candles blow out as he crosses the room. One by one. Each step casts a new web of darkness.

"Peter!" I call out, my voice heavy with desperation.

He stops just before the last bit of light is snuffed out. There is no gust, no breeze that would extinguish the fire. Nothing to make sense of the darkness coming for me.

The hackles on my arms and the back of my neck stand on edge. I've never been this scared. It's an instinctual fear. A nagging feeling like the one I get walking into a parking garage by myself. I steady my racing heart. "Where am I?"

Pink and yellow light pours into the room from the windows. Not as bright as the sun rising, but that dim, in-between, hue where both the sun and moon are in the sky. It happens too fast for time to have changed and yet I can't deny what I'm seeing with my own eyes.

Peter looks over his shoulder. Shadows fall over half his face, cloaking him like a bandit in permeable darkness. "You're in Never-land, Darling."

CHAPTER 9
Wednesday

Peter doesn't shut the door when he leaves.

It's open, tempting me to run. Taunting me with the hope of freedom.

I've never been kidnapped but based on my limited experience on the matter, drawing from all the smutty stories I've read, I do not want to try to escape through that door. There's a good chance this opening is a trap or that someone is standing guard outside it waiting for me to do the obvious.

Yeah... not gonna happen.

Looking around the room, there's not much to see. The walls are bare, furniture minimal. The faint hue of a yellow light seeps from the hallway into my space. I don't think I'm on the first floor of the house. Kidnapper logic dictates the bedroom window should be blocked, maybe even barred. Truth be told, I'm surprised I'm not in a basement or chained to the bed, or... something.

Maybe I've read too many books.

I walk across the room, trying my hardest to keep the pitter-patter of my feet quiet. The house is still. Scarily so, without a single noise carrying into my room. I pad to the window and stare at the world outside, even more baffled.

This is a treehouse.

A literal, sitting on limbs, made from wood, surrounded by leaves, treehouse. What the fuck?

Rope bridges connect this house to more tiny log cabins, crossing over and through I don't even know how many trees. Oaks, pines, and laurels intertwine to shield the houses in dense foliage. All of which are at least ten feet off the ground. I can't say for certain how many houses there are but it's a good number.

More than a handful.

Which makes me wonder how many people Peter has under his thumb. How many women has he kidnapped over the years?

Most importantly, what does he do with the girls?

My throat goes dry at the thoughts running through my mind. People don't live in groups like this by choice. There has to be some incentive, something Peter can offer them. Fresh meat for the men to dip their sticks in. I chew on my bottom lip, letting it all sink in. So long as this isn't a Dahmer-type compound, I'll be okay.

I've got this.

Sure, being kidnapped by a possibly crazy hottie isn't ideal, but all the great romances start off this way. Maybe Peter will be the broody possessive type and not want to share. I'll take that over the alternative.

I rack my brain, trying to think of some stories I've read with the forced proximity trope. The first one that pops into my head is *ACOTAR*. Tampon, I mean Tamlin, and Feyre had a good run. He stole her away first, and then her fairy mate forced her into spending time with him, but it all worked out in the end.

Hades and Persephone are another good one. They eventually fell in love after a whirlwind adventure... so to speak.

Uhh... my mind draws a blank after those two, but I'm sure there are more success stories out there. I know I've read more. I will be fine! *Keep telling yourself this, Wens.*

On the bright side, I don't see any lights. All of the windows are dark, which makes me wonder what time it is. The in-between hues of the day give me hope that everyone is either sleeping or working.

I chew on my lip, debating whether to make a run for it tonight or wait and see what I'm being forced into. There are downfalls to both scenarios, but I wager that I have a small advantage right now.

Peter thinks I'm weak, probably too tired and scared to make a move. I'll only have the element of surprise once. Now is the best chance I've got. If I get caught, I can adjust my strategy and try again another time. I just wish my only option wasn't the window.

I hate heights.

The lock on the glass is ancient and pushes the frame open instead of sliding upwards. Carefully I lift the latch that holds it shut, terrified it'll make a noise. I let out a small, triumphant breath when it's unlocked and look over my shoulder.

No one is watching me.

No one heard the click of metal letting loose.

I reign in my excitement. The cynic in me insists something will go wrong with my plan. Be it now or once I'm on the ground running, I need to be prepared for the worst.

But that doesn't stop me from hoping for the best.

I press my hand against the cedar window frame. Slowly, carefully, I push it open. The hinges squeak. In a normal house, the sound would barely be heard over the whoosh of a running air conditioning and the little noises of life being lived. Here... it's too quiet.

"There's a front door, you know."

I freeze at the sound of a male voice. It's different from Peter's. Lighter. Not so baritone. The man behind me chuckles. Heavy steps echo off the walls. I swallow the lump in my throat and stand up taller. He doesn't know I planned to run.

I was hot.

I opened a window.

End of story.

I turn to face the intruder and lose all train of thought. Eyes the color of maple leaves in the fall drag over my body, making me aware that I am still in Tyle's string bikini. My hair is probably a matted mess, my makeup running and ruined. For a second I hope he isn't scared off by my appearance, then mentally scold myself for caring. Captor number two may be a nineties DiCaprio replica, but he is not a love interest. End of story!

My new warden takes his time, drinking in my curves while I shamelessly admire the outline of his body. Even in the dim light I can see his shirt stretched across his pecs. Tan, or maybe brown, cargo shorts hang low on his hips. I bite the corner of my lip and come up with a new plan.

Divide and conquer by any means possible.

If I can get this beautiful creature on my side, I can learn about Peter and the island. Find some leverage and then get the hell out of here.

"You, Darling, are going to give Peter a run for his money."

I lean against the open window sill and arch my back. The girls, still wet from my unwanted swimming adventure, probably shine like headlights through the sheer cover-up.

Mr. DiCaprio looks, unashamed of his gaze falling to my chest. Excitement shoots through me. I have two dream-worthy men under one roof, one of who checks every box on the panty-dropping list and the other who's a bad decision waiting to happen. Both of which look like they'd be a wild ride. These are dangerous waters. "Is that so?"

Blondie wiggles a sandwich filled zip lock baggie in the air and then tosses it on the bed. "I thought you might be hungry after your journey. Coming to Neverland can take a lot out of a girl."

My stomach growls in response. I don't know how long it's been since I last ate. I had lunch by the pool with the bridesmaids, but that was hours ago, if not longer. "What is it?"

"Peanut butter and jelly," he declares as if it's the best sandwich in the world.

Oh. Damn. I can't eat that, but do the islanders know about my allergy? Are they actively trying to finish what Peter started? Or is this sheer coincidence? "How do I know it's not poison?"

"There's no fun in killing you, Darling." He taps the tip of my nose as he says the nickname Peter coined.

I think the statement is supposed to be reassuring, but all I hear is the unspoken yet. The lingering promise of torment, even if it's only a never-ending longing to go home.

"Peter has bigger plans for you." He chuckles and walks to the edge of the bed and grabs the sandwich out of the bag. He takes a bite, not waiting to swallow before asking, "Am I dead yet?"

I fight a smile and cross my arms. I don't know what to make of this guy. Peter is all broody and blah while his new warden is rainbows and sunshine. Talk about emotional whiplash. "Doesn't seem like it, but the jury's still out. It could be slow-acting poison."

Dude smirks and extends the sandwich to me. "Then we die together. What do you say? Be the Capulet to my Montague?" He laughs again. A deep belly rumbling chuckle. "I'm joking. It's just a sandwich. You've had a long day. You should eat something."

"Can't. I'm allergic to peanut butter." I shrug.

"Oh, shit. Really?!" he stammers, all playfulness gone. "I'm sorry."

He runs out of the room, baggie, and sandwich in hand. A door kicks down the hall, probably hanging against a wall.

I stand there, waiting to see if he comes back. I mean, who does that...just leaves mid-conversation.

Blondie returns back a couple of minutes later with two glasses of pink juice. He hands me one, a serious apologetic look on his face. "I brushed my teeth, just in case you're like allergic allergic."

His minty breath makes me want to smile again. This guy is tumbling through my defenses with his charm and I've barely known him for five minutes. I need to batten down the hatches and prepare my lady bits for war. This is a game of skill, with a high possibility of a bedroom romp. There's no time for butterflies or any of that bullshit. "I mean, I am, but only if I eat it".

"Good to know. I'm Casper, but everybody here calls me Cass." He folds one arm over his stomach and bows while extending his other arm outward.

The gesture reminds me of the ringmaster at a circus I went to once when I was a kid. That man had the same exaggerated move-ment, the kind meant for putting on a show. I'm sure that's all this is. A show of deceptive trust to lure me into a false sense of safety. Well, two can play his game.

"Wednesday." I bring the cup to my nose and sniff. The pink stuff smells sour like lemonade, but also sweet. "Is this gonna kill me too?"

"A bit paranoid, aren't you?" Cass chuckles again. There's a hint of mischievous playfulness in his question, the kind you expect a twelve-year-old to have with every word that comes out their mouth, not a twenty-something year old.

"Humor me. Peter tried to kill me and then kidnapped me when I survived. And now I've got you, a new player on the board, bringing me food and drink not even five minutes after he tells me I'm stuck, and I quote, in Neverland. Can you blame me if I'm on edge about everything?" "

"Fair point." Cass takes my cup and downs half of the juice, pink at the bottom and yellow on top, in one big swallow. He holds up one finger as he swallows, keeping us in a suspended state of silence even after he's done. "Nope, not dead. I think it is safe to say that this drink here." He points at my glass. "Is not going to kill you."

"You're lucky you're cute." I lift my cup and take a sip. The flavor is unlike anything I've ever had before...in a good way. It's sweet and tangy and burns my throat going down, but it's delicious. I didn't realize how thirsty I was. My stomach grumbles again, reminding me that it too is needy. "What is this?"

"Cloudberry lemonade."

"I've never heard of it."

"The cloudberries are only grown on the island and in two regions of the world. Although somehow one of your chain restaurants has managed to mass produce it and sell their lemonade during your summers." He pauses, staring off into space before mumbling, "I need to have Emmit look into that."

"Who's Emmit?"

"My brother. You know..." Cass walks over to the window and stares out. I can't see the sky from here. There are too many trees, but I imagine it's clear and the evening stars are just beginning to poke through.

The simplicity of knowing that I'm under the same shifting sky as Kenny is comforting. It shouldn't be. I shouldn't be thinking about my cheating ex, but that's the problem with love. When it's true, the heart never lets go. There will always be memories and triggers to remind you of what you've lost. Moments when you find comfort in the past, no matter how painful the present is.

"Are you thirsty?" Cass asks, suddenly.

I wiggle my nearly empty glass in the air.

He rolls his eyes, laughing again. "Not what I was talking about. Come on."

Cass hops onto the windowsill like a spider monkey. He crouches, extending one foot out onto the roof, and holds his hand out for me.

I hesitate, my fear of heights trickling into my consciousness. Leaving this room sounds great, but not out of that death trap. "I thought you said there was a front door?"

"Where's your sense of adventure, Darling?"

"Back home, with all the clothes I'm not wearing." I gesture to the barely-there bikini.

"I'm not complaining." Cass winks.

I roll my eyes because that's such a guy thing to say. The normalcy of his comment is a good distraction. My mind has gone off the deep end, drawing up ways I could fall to my demise once we step outside.

Cass laughs, apparently amused by my reaction. "Fine. Fine. I know someone who's about your size. She'll have something you can borrow." He wiggles his fingers and glances down at his outstretched palm. "What do you say, Darling? Are you ready for your first adventure in Neverland?"

No, but this is what I wanted, help out of the treehouse and someone with an in to give me information. Match that with Cass's lust-filled eyes and I'd say my plan is already in motion. I just wish there was another, safer way out of here.

CHAPTER 10
Wednesday

W e scale the roof and jump down onto a platform. I hold in my nerves and follow Cass. Step by step. I don't have a problem with heights. It's the falling part that makes me nervous. I kind of wish this was Neverland. At least then I could hold on to the happy thought of being free and fly if I slip.

The roof is easy. It's solid. Steady. It's the next part of our journey that makes me want to turn back and wait for another opening to present itself.

Rope bridges connect one treehouse to another. The planks are secured with loops on each end and that's it. There are no handrails to hold onto, no supports to offset the rhythm of movement. The boards wobble and tilt with each step, throwing me off balance.

Walking on them by myself might not be bad, but Cass's extra weight makes going from one house to the next near impossible.

I drop down to my hands and knees after the first half-dozen steps. Crawling seems safer. I can grip the boards with my fingers. I close my eyes and try to trick my brain into thinking I'm on solid ground as I inch forward.

Cass is rambling, probably telling me things about Neverland I should be listening to but all I can hear is the sound of my heart in my ears. Thump. Thump. Deafeningly loud.

"Woman." He sighs.

I look up. Cass has made it to the next platform while I'm still somewhere in between Peter's treehouse and where I'm supposed to be. Cass shakes his head and jogs back to me. The bridge wobbles from side to side, tilting me to the left and right. Left and right.

I take a slow steady breath. If I focus on my breathing I can regulate my heart rate. Once I get that back to normal, I can make it across the bridge to something solid.

"You're gonna get us caught if we go this slow." Cass crouches low, turning his back to me. "Get on."

"You've got to be joking." I try to laugh but it sounds like a strangled cry.

Cass looks over his shoulder. Hazel eyes meeting mine. "Afraid not, Darling, and I'd like to be thoroughly inebriated by the time Peter figures out you've left the room. So..." He taps his back.

A barrage of what could go wrong streams through my mind, but that's not what makes me pause. It's the thought of relying on a person I'm not sure I can trust and the temptation of being that close to someone who is my kryptonite. I know, that's the last place my mind should be, but trauma does weird things to the brain. I hesitate, refusing to crawl the remaining inches.

"Come on, Darling," Cass whispers. He looks around, his gaze bouncing to two of the treehouses in front of us, like he's about to tell me a secret, before finding my gaze again. "We both know you want to ride me."

I laugh and the knot of stress in my chest releases. "You're insufferable."

Cass winks because in his mind that is an acceptable rebuttal. I give in and climb on his back. He's solid, all muscle between my legs. Strong fingers grip my thighs. I wrap my arms around his neck and unintentionally breathe him in. He smells like the forest, like earth and pines with a hint of vanilla. It's nice.

He carries me to the first platform and then across two more bridges before setting me down on the doorstep of a small treehouse. I'm dizzy from how fast my heart is racing but grateful. I don't think I could have made it down the bridges by myself.

"Is this your place?" I ask, curious to see what's hidden in his closets both metaphorically and physically.

I can't decide what to think about Cass yet. He's got the same playfulness that Peter had on the boat...before pushing me overboard. The kind that makes me want to smile and forget the reality of my situation. But then there's the serious side of him that clashes with his personality.

He doesn't seem too keen on Peter, which is a win in my book. If they aren't buddy-buddy, driving a wedge between them should be cake. Especially once I spread my legs for him. I've already decided it's going to happen. Even if it doesn't help my cause, he's the second hottest man I've ever met. I have high hopes he can put my vibrator to shame in the orgasm department and will be sorely disappointed if I'm wrong.

"I'd rather cut my left nut off than live with this woman." He scoffs, turning the handle.

The door isn't locked, which makes me wonder about the rest of the treehouses. Once I figure out who I'm dealing with, I might be able to break into one and find some leverage. I'm not beneath blackmailing someone if it'll help me get home.

"Come on." Cass lights a lantern by the door and carries it with him across the open room.

I stay close behind and take in every detail. There's not much to see inside. A small couch. A table and chairs. There's nothing on the walls. No pictures of friends or family. At this rate, blackmail might be harder than I thought.

Cass stops in front of a door and opens it. He goes straight to the dresser, like he's been here before, and rummages through the drawers.

I sit on the full-size bed. This room is similar to the one Peter had me in, with the same bare necessities. Dresser. Bed. Nightstand with an oil lamp. The only difference is the layout. The rooms are flipped.

"Try these on." Cass tosses me a pair of jean shorts and a white shirt that has a raven on it.

I step into the shorts and pull them over my hips. They're tight. I can't button them, but they are high enough on my waist that they won't fall down either.

Cass watches me. Hungry eyes drinking in every inch of exposed skin. "We'll need to find you something better, but those should work for tonight."

"Does Neverland have a mall?" I'm joking. I have yet to see anything resembling the twenty-first century in either treehouse. No refrigerator. No stove or tv. Hell, the rooms don't even have a light. I doubt the shopping is up to par.

"The pirate's market has just about everything."

"Pirates?" I pull the shirt over my head. It has cutouts on the sides, but it's not too revealing. Better than walking around half-naked all night, I suppose. "Like in the stories?"

"What stories?"

"You know of Peter Pan, the boy who doesn't grow up. Captain Hook. Tinkerbell and the Lost Boys." I pull my hair into a ponytail with the tie on my wrist. Cass is looking at me like I have two heads. I don't like it. "What?"

He steps forward and takes both my hands in his. "Promise me you won't tell anyone what you just told me, Wednesday."

"Oh...kay. Why? The story is like a hundred years old. Everyone knows it."

Cass frowns and shakes his head. "Not everyone. I would bet my life none of The Lost know that story exists. If anyone found out..." He chews on the corner of his lip. "They just can't. Please, Wednesday. I'm begging you."

"All right. I promise. But you owe me."

"Anything, Darling." He squeezes my hands tight and then sets them free. "Name it and it's yours."

"For starters, you can stop calling me Darling. It's creepy. My friends call me Wens."

"Bless the stars, she considers me a friend!" Cass wraps his arms around my waist. He spins me around once, then sets me on my feet, an infectious grin lifting his lips at the corners. "Come on. We have about an hour or so until Peter rears his ugly face. I need a drink or ten before that happens. What do you say?"

"I'd say a drink sounds like heaven about now."

"Well, my lady, your chariot awaits." Cass turns his back to me and crouches low again.

I laugh and climb onto his back.

Neverland, here I come.

CHAPTER 11
Wednesday

I t's official, nature is not my friend.

Her leaves are pokey, her roots raised specifically for tripping, and she's filled with bloodsucking creepy crawlies that seem to only drink O-negative blood. Thank heavens for my sneakers. If I would have been in heels or flats before nearly dying this afternoon, I would be screwed.

"Maybe this was a bad idea." We stop at the edge of the tree line, just out of reach of the firelight. There are about a dozen people gathered near a bonfire in the sand. Most of them stand around the flames, listening to music my parents grew up on from an eighty-style boombox.

"Worried I'll run away?" I tease, but the idea has been looming in my mind. The only thing stopping me is I have no idea where I am. The woods are a maze, with no defining markers.

Cass's chuckle sends a flutter rolling over my skin. "Are you that eager to get away from me, Darling?"

Cass specifically? No. I like him, even though I know I shouldn't. It's easy to forget the gravity of my situation when we're together. His lighthearted, playfulness erases all the worry and dread weighing on my heart. But the fact of the matter is that if there was a chance for me to get away, I'd take it. I'd leave all the warm-fuzzy feelings in a heartbeat if it meant I could go home.

"Worried?"

"Of course!" Cass takes my hand and twirls me around, pulling me into him in one swift movement. "Half those fuckers will try to steal you from me the moment I walk away, and I'm not ready to let you go yet."

"Who said I was yours?" I ask, unsure of the signals I want to send.

I've seen Tyle use men to get what she wants, and it's always ended with the guy getting hurt. The guilt that I'm doing the same with Cass doesn't sit well in my soul. That and Peter still lingers in my thoughts, even though I wish he wouldn't.

Disappointment passes across Cass's face. The reaction is brief and gone as quick as it came, replaced by a flash of teeth. "No one, but I want you to be mine because you're gorgeous and your soul burns brighter than any star in the sky."

My cheeks heat, a smile tugging at my lips. I've never heard anyone say something so beautifully odd before.

Cass takes my hand, not pushing the conversation further, and leads us out to the party. My converse sink in the loose sand. I don't feel nervous when the first set of eyes land on us, or even the second. It's the third, fourth, and fifth that make my heart race. I wiggle my fingers and try to pull my hand back. Cass takes the hint, sensing my social anxiety. He sets me free but stays close, wordlessly claiming me as his.

"Who's this?" The voice comes from one of the men near a wooden corn hole board. I'm not sure which one. All of them are looking at me with a mix of curiosity and lust. Four shirtless bodies stare, each one just as beautifully muscled as the next, watching my every move.

"The new darling." A girl with a *we don't do well with strangers* expression says. She crosses her arms, glaring as she takes in my appearance. "Your ass is too big for those shorts."

"Stars and Scars, Heidi. You were new once. Ease up." A pretty Hispanic with long dark hair, in cutoff jeans and a gray tank-top, nudges the first girl—Heidi— with her elbow. "I'm Aria and this is Scarlett."

"Wednesday," I say, trying to seem friendly even though my guard is up. Are these more kidnappers? Or people Peter has stolen and brainwashed?

Cass jerks his chin to the guys and rambles off their names in one breath. I don't know who is who. No one waves or gives any signal for me to match a name to a face. They just stare, a few sipping on their mason jar glasses, like they couldn't care less I'm here. I almost wonder if the boys do it on purpose. So I can't identify them to the police when I finally make it home.

"I need to take care of some business. You gonna be okay on your own for a few minutes?" Cass asks.

I look up at him, realizing that his height seems to be the norm and my five-foot-five stature is small, even by the girl's standards. Their legs are long, their bodies lean. I'm short, with a few extra pounds here and there. Insecurity bleeds into my soul. Tyle was always thinner than me, strikingly beautiful like these girls.

And I'm just... me.

It makes me nervous to be left alone with these people but I put on a mask of confidence. Fear can be manipulated, used to make someone do stupid, reckless things. I may be shaking in my converse, but this isn't my first rodeo. I can fake it with the best of them. "I'm a big girl. Don't worry about me."

Cass flashes his teeth. "It's not you that I'm worried about." He leaves me to myself and heads to talk to the group of guys by the fire.

One of them, a dirty blonde, holds my gaze the longest. I can't help but notice the similarities between him and Cass. Same nose. Same kiss me lips and dimpled smile. I'm guessing he's the brother Cass mentioned.

"You're going to get Casper in trouble," Scarlett, the Asian chick beside Aria, whispers. Her gaze darts to Heidi, who nods in encouragement, before she adds, "You shouldn't encourage him."

"Maybe I want to cause a little trouble." I smirk, feeling triumphant to have figured something out. Peter has a jealous side. Good. I'll kill two birds with one stone with Cass.

I sit beside Scarlett on the picnic bench and watch Cass's features morph from the playful boyish spirit I've spent most of the evening with to a serious one. I hate to admit watching him kind of turns me on. He checks every box on my fuck-them-without-second-thought list. Assuming he swings his dick with the same confidence he talks to his friends with, I won't have to fake it when I seduce him later.

"Oh, boy," a feminine voice, I think Aria says. I turn to her as she smiles against the rim of her jar, taking a sip of a powder-blue drink.

"What?"

"Nothing." She glances across the sandy knoll to the men and their meeting. "I just know that look."

"And?" I don't have a look. I'm tempted to tell her as much, but I get the feeling she wants to stir the pot. There can't be much to enter-tain people here. I don't know how big Neverland is, but I haven't seen power lines or anything resembling the twenty-first century.

Aria tilts her head, her grin stretching wider. "It means that we all need to be shit-faced before Peter discovers you're catching feelings for Cass. You drink, new girl?"

"Sometimes." I try to mask my reservations. I don't do a good job.

Heidi stares at me for a moment, distrust dancing across her features as she studies me. "How did you say you got to Neverland?"

"I didn't."

Cass returns in the knick of time, with two wooden cups in his hands. I hide a breath of relief. I don't want anyone to know too much about me. Anything I give these people could be used to track me down again after I escape.

"Causing trouble?" he teases.

"Not yet," Aria answers with a wink. She seems to be the friendliest of the bunch. Heidi has done nothing but throw daggers with her eyes at me, and Scarlett has barely looked up from her hands. They're an odd bunch. In the outside world, I doubt they'd be friends yet somehow on this island they work. "But I've got a feeling mischief is brewing just beyond the horizon."

"Most definitely." Cass's dark eyes trail my every movement. Every tiny shift of my weight and blink of my eyes.

The intensity of his gaze makes me shiver. Peter gave me the same nervous butterflies and he turned out to be a murderous creep. How do I know Cass isn't just as twisted? The pretty boys are the most dangerous, and I have a feeling the ones on this island bring a different kind of peril.

"Thanks." I sniff the sparkly pink drink before tasting it. It smells sweet, like something I would order from a bar which causes me to hesitate. How did Cass know I'd want a fruity drink and not something with some bite?

"Scared, new girl?" Heidi taunts, pure venom dripping from her tone. Her lips lift into a sinister smile.

I roll my eyes and bring the cup to my lips then take a swallow. The drink tastes like cotton candy, pure sweetness without a hint of bite. It's the kind of cocktail that sneaks up on you, gives you a good time until you find yourself puking over a bush an hour later. "What is this?"

"Faery Wine."

I smile, my lips lifting on their own, and welcome the way the wine melts away my resolve. I was wrong. The wine isn't sneaky. It packs a punch straight out the gate and hits my nerves after the first taste.

The buzz flitters through my whole body. It's a flying kind of feeling that enhances every touch. I feel the wind caress my skin. I feel grains of sand tickle my toes and the pink light of both day and night bathe me in its glory. Each new sensation is better than the last. I take another sip, a bigger one this time, desperate for more.

"Easy, Wens." Cass frowns, his copper brows pulling together. "This is a sipping drink. Enjoy the ride." He takes the glass from my hands and sets it on the table and links his fingers with mine. "Dance with me."

"Crazy For You" by Madonna croons through the old boom box. Cass twirls me once then pulls me into his hard chest. I stumble, my feet two steps behind me. He compensates for my missteps and holds me tighter, ensuring I don't fall on my face. We sway, taking tiny steps in the sand.

"I've waited centuries for you, Wednesday," he whispers, the tip of his nose brushing against my neck, just under my ear.

"That's nice," I mumble, the words a distance ping in my mind.

I close my eyes and let Cass guide me, giving him total control of my body. The world is a swirly haze of music and emotions. This wine is potent. I only had a few sips and I can feel every chord sung out by the speakers vibrate against my skin.

Cass's lips press against mine, tenderly asking permission to deepen the kiss. I want to open my mouth and let myself fall head first into this drunken headiness, but my mind won't let me. It strays to Peter and what it felt like to be in this same position only hours ago.

I like Cass. I like how he makes me forget I've been kidnapped. I like how each breath I take around him is light and the longer we're together the less bitter I feel about being here.

But he's not the blue-eyed madman who set my world on fire. A man I hate so deeply yet can't seem to erase the imprint he left on my soul.

"Am I interrupting?" Peter's voice rumbles.

"Uh oh." Heidi snickers.

I open my eyes, pissed that not only is Peter fucking with my mind but he's here, physically cock-blocking me. I glare at him over Cass's shoulder, inwardly pleased at the scowl on his face. "As a matter of fact, you are."

"I need a word," Peter demands. He crosses his arms over the loose fitting tee that covers his chest.

If I look hard enough I can see the dark lines of his tattoos. I remember tracing them, touching his smooth skin, the way lust shot to my center. My nipples harden beneath my shirt, the same needy heat pooling again. "I'm busy."

"It's not a request."

"Considering that I don't belong to you, I don't care." I step out of Cass's hold and take his hand.

I'm frustrated, and not just sexually. How dare Peter show up and demand I talk to him. He was the one to leave my room without giving me any answers! Chanting a stupid tick-tock rhyme that made as much sense as telling me I'm in Neverland. I march toward the tree line and drag Cass with me.

"Where are you going?" Peter demands.

"To finish what you so rudely interrupted," I say reactively. I stomp over fallen limbs, purposefully trying to make as much noise as I can.

"Wednesday!" Peter shouts.

"Can't hear you!" I march and march, taking us deeper into the woods. My stupid lady bits are dripping with need. Arguing with Peter is almost as much of a turn on as touching him is which only makes me angrier. I don't want to be attracted to that psychopath!

"Where are we going?" Cass asks, not bothering to hide his amusement.

I stop in the middle of the woods. I was so lost in my thoughts, I almost forgot I'd drug him into my mess. I look around, not recognizing a single thing around me, and sigh. "I don't know."

The fire from the party faintly glows through the brush behind us. I half expected Peter to stomp after me in a man-fit, demanding I do what he says, but he just let me go. I don't know why, but I'm disappointed.

"Want to come back to my place?" Cass asks. There's no innuendo in his question. I can't tell if he's being genuinely nice or hoping I'll make good on my word.

I glance over my shoulder, still hoping Peter will storm through the trees and drag me away kicking and screaming. I give him three heartbeats before deciding he must be calling my bluff.

If Peter thinks I'm not going to screw Cass, he's got another thing coming. I'm going to scream so loud that everyone on the island will blush from embarrassment. I want to douse that tiny spark of jealousy with gasoline and watch his world burn.

I trail my gaze over Cass's lean body, noting the way his shirt falls over the muscles of his chest. This may be a show for Peter, but that doesn't mean it won't be fun. "Lead the way."

CHAPTER 12
Wednesday

ass's treehouse smells like a garden. Aromas of greenery and jasmine and sage, mixed with the sweet scent of flora fills the air.

He turns the knob of an oil lantern as we step inside, lighting the small space. Unlike the other two rooms I've been in, there is no table or chairs in the main room. Books upon books lie in stacks on the floor while trinkets fill his shelves.

"Are you thirsty?" He walks to the kitchen counter while I make my way to the shelves that line the walls. The oddities are chaotic. A button. A watch. A deflated red balloon. Toy car. An empty matchbook. Every item is broken in some fashion and yet he keeps them.

"What is all of this?"

I turn around. Cass has two cups in his hands. I shake my head, uninterested in whatever he has to offer. The faery wine is wearing off. There's a pounding behind my eye that's getting stronger the longer I stand in the light.

"Pieces of people." He sets both glasses on the counter and strides toward me. His fingers graze my hips. "Things that washed up on the shore over the years. Little moments from someone's life they once cherished, now forgotten."

"How are your hands so cold?" I shiver, wondering what they'd feel like around my neck. I've always liked ice in the bedroom, the way it awakens the nerves and enhances an orgasm.

"Forever frost," Cass whispers into my ear. He pulls me backward and presses my ass against him. His breath caresses my skin. His lips less than an inch away. "It coats the inside of the pitcher."

"I've never heard of it." I arch my back and press into the hardness on my thigh.

Cass reaches up and wraps his fingers around my neck. I groan, thrilled he has the same desires as I do. He turns me around, controlling my every move, and looks me in the eyes. "You'd never heard of cloudberries either before tonight, and yet you've drunk their lemonade."

"Is this why you brought me here? To tell me about ice that never melts and sober me up some." I touch Cass' chest. My fingers run between the muscles of his pecs and down his abs. I want him more than I should for reasons that make me blush. Selfish, dirty reasons that are as shallow as I want to come to the deviousness of I hope Peter finds out what I've done.

Cass's breath hitches. He inches closer. "Are you sure this is a good idea?"

No. I run my fingers through his hair and pull his mouth to mine. My first thought is of Peter and how his tongue is more skilled, but he's gone from my mind the minute Cass's hand slides up my shirt.

He cups my breast and squeezes until my eyes pop open. He's rough, which is what I need because I need to be punished. What I'm doing is wrong on so many levels. But it feels. So. Good. I moan against his lips, the pain a direct link to my lady bits.

Cass lifts me onto the counter and I wrap my legs around his hips. He pulls away to yank his shirt over his head and then he's on me again.

He tugs the strings of my bikini loose. It falls to my lap, discarded and my shirt rises up by my shoulders. He sucks my left breast into his mouth, teeth nipping at my puckered nipple, while his finger massages the sensitive flesh of my other one.

I drop my head back, unfazed by the thunk it makes as I hit the counters.

"Wednesday," Cass breathes, against my skin. "We should stop."

"I don't want to." I try to lift his face to mine, to make his lips stop talking with my own, but he pulls away.

"You're drunk. I don't want you to regret this tomorrow."

Warmth pools in my heart. It figures I would find the only gentleman in the world on an island I'm trying to escape from. Guilt that I'm using him to make Peter jealous rears its ugly head.

I should walk away and find somewhere safe to sleep tonight, but I need Peter to hear my screams echoing through the trees. I want Cass to be the man to satisfy me because he's hot and I think we would enjoy each other. But I won't force him to do anything he's uncomfortable with.

"Stop being such a gentleman, Cass. Either you make me feel good tonight or I'll find somebody who will."

Cass doesn't hesitate. His mouth crashes against mine again. Strong hands slide under my ass, lifting me in the air. Cass carries me to the bedroom. His lips pepper my shoulder, teeth nip my ear as he kicks a door open.

The room we're in is dark and I'm too into the moment to take in the scenery. He drops me on the bed. I take off my shirt and shorts and toss them to the floor.

Cass is on top of me, equally as bare, and kisses my lips. Neck. Shoulder. The triangle of my bikini bottom is pulled aside. He dips a finger between my folds while sucking my nipple into his mouth.

Cass's hand squeezes me again. He toys with me, giving me as much pleasure as he can without letting me come, keeping me just behind the line until my hips buck. I'm panting, greedy, wanting more of whatever he'll give me.

It doesn't take long for him to take the hint and align himself with my center. Through the lusty haze, I remind him, "Condom," before he can push himself inside me.

"I can't get you pregnant," he says, lips a breath beneath my ear.

"I've heard that before." I arch my eyebrows. He can't honestly think I'm stupid enough to fall for that line.

"Scared your birth control won't work?"

I push on Cass's chest. He shifts onto his side and somehow there's not a single roll of fat on his body. Mine would have wrinkled and looked disgusting in that position. "How'd you know I'm taking birth control?"

He traces the thin line on the inside of my arm. The scar is only visible thanks to the tan I got in the Keys.

"I like covering my bases." He presses his lips to the sweet spot on my neck. "Kids aren't in the future for me, Wens. Even if you weren't protected, I'm sterile."

My eyes flutter closed. It's been a long time since someone made me feel this good. The need and what's left of the wine gnaws away at my restraint. I slide my hand between us and angle my hips. His perfect, heart-shaped tip slides inside me. Cass finishes pushing himself in. I gasp as my skin stretches to accommodate his thickness.

Cass kisses my neck, letting me have a minute to adjust. He starts slow, taking his time to enjoy my tightness. It's been months since I've let anyone down there and almost two weeks since I've touched myself thanks to red week and the bachelorette party. I'm gasping within minutes, ready to come. I writhe underneath him, unable to control myself as an orgasm rocks my body.

"Sweet, fuck," Cass mumbles as he thrusts deeper inside me. His release isn't far off and he finishes with a long, loud grunt.

Cass rolls off me and walks to a room I'm assuming is a bathroom. I lay on the bed, breathless, covered in sweat. His warm seed drips out of me. I cringe, disgusted with myself. I've never let a man come inside me before. That's always been my stipulation. They either had to wear a condom or pull out. I wanted to save this one thing for my future life partner, and I let my ego and hormones ruin the only precious thing I had to give.

"You okay?" Cass tosses me a wet washcloth.

I wipe my lady bits then sit up. Hopefully gravity will pull whatever is left inside of me out so I can pretend this never happened. "Getting clingy already?" I deflect.

"I'd be a fool not to." Cass leans down and cups my neck then tilts my head upward to plant a kiss to my lips. "You are a treasure, Wednesday. I'm not ashamed to admit I want you all to myself."

My heart flutters, elated to have such beautiful words spoken to me. I'm sure they're fake. Men don't mean such treasured things after only knowing someone for a few hours. Still, Cass makes me feel special.

If only my head would stop wishing the words had come from Peter's mouth.

CHAPTER 13
Wednesday

I wake in a bed that is not my own, in a room that is too bright.

The sun shines through curtainless windows, painting wooden walls in hues of pale pink and yellow. For one beautiful moment, I forget everything that's happened in the last twenty-four hours. But as I push myself upwards on a crisp, white bedsheet with no blankets, everything comes back with painful recognition.

My head hurts a little, the aftermath of drinking too much, but overall I feel fine. Well, as fine as I can be considering the situation.

"Mornin'." Cass leans against the doorframe, a white t-shirt falling just below the band of his khaki shorts. He looks good with a shirt on, but even better without it. I fight a frown, remembering all the things we did last night.

I don't feel bad about sleeping with him. My body is my temple and he worshiped it better than anyone has before, man or woman. I only wish I hadn't been so stupid as to let him come inside me. The gift I had for my life partner is lost.

As pretty as Cass is, things between us will never be long term. He is a means to piss off Peter and pass the time. Possibly even help me find a way home. And I am the new girl. Someone he can have a little fun with as long as we stay casual.

That's all.

"Hey." My voice is scratchy from all the yelling. At least I managed to do one thing right last night.

"Thirsty?" he asks. I nod, and Cass brings me the cup he's holding. A small wooden thing, whittled from what looks to have been a thick tree limb. The bark carefully peeled off, inside hollowed. "Careful, it's warm."

The cup is neither hot nor cold in my hands, but I'm careful to bring its contents to my lips. Heat rises to my nose, along with the smell of honey and something floral. I doubt his tea will pack the caffeine punch I'm used to getting from coffee but it tastes surprisingly good. "Thanks."

"Has anyone ever told you how beautiful you look in the morning?" Cass stares at me, a glimmer of hope and a whole bunch of unspoken emotions I don't want to deal with shining in his eyes.

"Has anyone ever told you that your flattery balances a thin line between sweet and obsessive?"

"Does it bother you?"

"Surprisingly, no." I'm shocked as the words leave my lips, but even more taken back as I realize they ring true. It's kind of nice having someone be kind to me after they've gotten down my string bikini. Kenny's chivalry faded out after the one-year marker and one-night stands aren't known for hanging out once the deed is done.

Cass is the first hookup to stick around. He could have disappeared or sent Peter to come fetch me to get me out of his hair. Instead, he's here. I guess it wouldn't hurt to be nice.

"Just saying though, if you end up stalking me or become one of those obsessive weirdos, I know a guy who likes to...you know..." I run my thumb across my neck and give him a murderous glare.

Cass laughs, not the least bit intimidated by my threat. In all honesty, I doubt Peter would do anything to harm him. I have a feeling they're friends or at least bygones. But it sounded semi-decent as I said it.

"Peter isn't usually so dubious." Cass leans forward. His thick fingers clutch the footboard, his forearm muscles flexing with each shift of his weight. "When he's not fighting his demons, he's an all right guy."

"Your definition of all right and mine are different."

Cass smirks, and I find that sober me enjoys the shape of his mouth as much as drunk me did. "Just wait, Wednesday. You'll see the side of him we all do. It just takes time."

"That's something I don't have a lot of, Cass. Time." Something punches me in the stomach. Regret... maybe? It feels a lot like regret but I shake it off and chalk the sensation up to a hangover. I don't have the energy to deal with emotions like that. "I'm leaving the first chance I can. Whatever you want this thing between us to be... it's got a short shelf life."

Cass takes my hand. He flips it palm up and traces the lines with his finger. It's alluring. I find myself fascinated by the simplest of things, like the rising and falling of his chest, and I'm anxious to hear him speak. I can't justify the need to stay by his side but it's there, running through my confusion and hesitations.

"One thing you should know about Neverland, Wens. Time is relative. Our days stretch on forever if you want them to, or they can end in an instant and night will rise. We're stuck in the same span of time, moving neither forward or backward while the world carries on without us. Forever in the twilight hours. You say what we have has a short shelf life, I say it has a life and that's good enough for me."

I shake my head, unable to fight the smile. Never have I heard a man speak with such heart or in so many riddles. It's flattering and confusing all at once. My mind feels drugged trying to make sense of it all. "You're unreal, Casper. Where did you come from?"

"A forgotten land called Wescroff, but my origin doesn't matter. What does matter is that you need something decent to wear." Cass releases my hand and the haziness in my mind clears. "As much as I love seeing you in all your glory, Peter would have my head if I let you out like that."

"Damn, so it's not a nudist island?" I stand, my girls and all their glory out on display. I don't have a stitch of clothes on.

Cass adjusts himself over his shorts. "At times maybe. But not when it comes to you." He tosses me a shirt and my cutoffs from last night. "The shower is over there if you want to freshen up. The water will flow once you step under it and there's a towel beneath the sink."

"Is it on a sensor?" I bend over to pick up my bathing suit.

"Something like that." Cass groans. His fingers grip the foot of the bed. Eyes narrowing on me. "Hurry up and get ready before I change my mind and keep you here with me all day."

The pirate's market isn't a market, but a series of shops along a long boardwalk that connect to docks that stretch into the bay. Each storefront is built the same, made out of thatch hutches with roofs crafted of dried palms.

Unlike Cass's treehouse, which is comfortably cool, the shops here are hot. Whatever system he and Peter used to aerate their treehouses needs to be shared with the pirates because I'm sweating.

"How's about this?" Cass holds up a tie-dye shirt with vinyl lettering that reads, Boyfriend wanted. Apply within.

I laugh and throw the first shirt I touch at his chest. The clothes are in heaps. Piles on top of piles, completely unorganized, set together with no rhyme or reason. It's fun looking through everything, but it is starting to eat at my anxiety.

"Would you say the position is filled then?" He winks and drops the shirt onto the pile nearest him.

I roll my eyes and go back to searching. So far I've found two pairs of shorts, a one-piece bathing suit, and a sundress that should fit. I'm still searching for some underwear or at the least another bikini to rotate the bottoms with. "Where does this stuff come from?"

Cass ties a coconut bra around his neck. It's too small for his muscular frame, falling nowhere near his chest, and puts a pink mouse-ear headband on with it. "The pirates call Neverland the Isle of the Lost."

"So you're saying all of this is stuff people misplaced?"

"I'm saying things are often forgotten once they make their way to Neverland. The people who lost what you hold don't even realize it's gone."

"That's sad."

"It is what it is." He tosses his headband back onto the stack. It gets buried amongst the masses, discarded again instead of finding a new life with us. "There's another shop by the pub we can try."

"Okay. Who do we pay?" I look around searching for a shopkeeper.

Cass shakes his head and takes my hand. "Human habits die hard. We don't pay for things that are already free."

He holds me close and guides us down the walk. I take in the scenery. Smoke billows out the chimney of a windowless shop. Music plays on a corner, flowing from a small guitar. Two men engage in a game of cards. Life is being lived on this side of Neverland. It gives me hope for some normalcy because I've only seen people party where we're from.

Cedar burns from somewhere around us. Not the chimney, that smells of spice and pork. This scent is different. It tickles in my brain, summoning a memory I can't quite place.

I look behind me for the origin, but the flavor fades. I look ahead of us and rise on my toes to see over the shoulders of the men in our path.

There's a large black hat with a red feather and a dark cloak over broad shoulders. Something in my chest comes alive, tingling with recognition. The man—I don't know why I'm assuming he's male, but it feels right in my soul—stops walking.

Cass is talking a mile a minute, probably giving me the backstory of these shops, or rambling about the bird perched on the roof across the way. I don't know. His words are garbled, lost down a tunnel along with my thoughts.

All I can see is the cedar-smelling man. All I can think about is how his scent wraps around my chest, drawing me closer.

He turns, looking around as if he too can sense me. Dark stubble covers the side of a strong jaw, curving to match a long scar that marks his cheek.

Cass grabs my arm and pulls me between two buildings. He pins me against the wall, pushing me so hard against the wood the back of my head hits. His lips are on mine before pain can register in my mind. His tongue hungrily pushes my mouth open, sweeping inside. Taking all thoughts about the Cedar-smelling man with him.

He kisses and kisses. Hands roaming up the side of my body. His fingers cup my breast and I'm thinking they're his favorite asset. He pushes his leg between mine and squeezes my chest until a moan leaves my lips. My legs shake, lust pouring out of me.

Cass pulls back. His breaths are short. His lungs just as deprived of oxygen as mine.

"What was that for?" I ask.

"It's been too long since I've felt those lips." He kisses my neck. I shiver with delight and he sinks his teeth into me, lightly nibbling.

"You're ridiculous." I laugh a flush of heat rising to my cheeks.

67

Need pools in my belly. I ache to be touched again. I take a deep breath and remind myself about who is using who. If Cass wants my body I'm happy to give it to him, but I need to keep my head clear. "What about my clothes"?

"Where we're going, you don't need any."

CHAPTER 14
Peter

"You've been busy."

"You know what they say about idle hands." Darling drops a canvas bag on the ground, at her feet, then falls into the chair beside the window. She picks up Cass's paperback, *Franken-stein*, flips to the description on the rear cover, then sets it down with a frown. "Why am I not surprised you're a horror fan?"

Her gaze bounces around the room, never staying on one thing for more than a few seconds before jumping to something else. My house is simple. Not as bare as some of The Lost, but less decadent than the others in our enclave.

I have a wall of shelving, filled with books that have shown up over the years. A small wooden table with two chairs to match. The end table and wingback by the window, and a handful of bowls on the counter that hold fruit.

I gave up on living possessions such as photos and decor ages ago, but I never could let go of the books. I don't read them. Reading was Wendy's passion, not mine, but each leather-bound novel reminds me of her.

Some of the books were found on the island. Those are the oldest, the ones Wendy hand-picked and read aloud to John and Michael when they were little. Others I collected once I figured out how to cross between the realms. All of them bring me back to little moments suspended in time.

At first, it was a way to keep Wendy with me after she was gone. Neverland makes you forget and I never wanted to forget her. Now, they sit on my shelves, collecting dust until Cass finds it in his heart to pick one up or clean them off.

I haven't forgotten, but sometimes remembering is its own punishment.

Wednesday's eyes finally settle on me. Chocolate brown with flecks of emerald and gold throughout. Uniquely Wendy. So much of the old soul penetrates through to her new life.

"Cass said I had to be here. Care to tell me why?" She crosses her arms, those pretty brown eyes narrowing.

"You sleep in my bed. Not his." I let years of frustration bleed into my voice. Anger at my father for arranging the marriage between Wendy and James when he knew I loved her. Bleeding admiration at Wendy's dedication to her vows. The constant ache, as if being stabbed, with every whisper, every gentle touch James placed upon her skin, and every skip of my heart for when she stole a glance at me. It was enough to drive a man to insanity and yet I lived for it.

It was better to be a bystander in her life, helplessly watching as she found happiness and fell in love with another than to deprive a deserving woman of my heart because I could never give that to someone else when it was still bound to another. I was content to die alone and love her from afar so long as she was happy.

"I'd rather sleep on the floor than with you!" Wednesday's venom matches mine.

I clench my teeth, refusing to let myself laugh. I love her spirit. The fight that burns through Wednesday's blood is instinctual. Ingrained in her DNA. But I have to focus on the negative feelings. I need to draw up the memories of Wendy's shaking breath as my brother screwed her in my bed because that is the only way I can stomach being so cruel. "That can be arranged, Darling."

"You're a pig." She rolls her eyes. "Why even bring me to this stupid island if you're going to be an ass, Peter?"

I didn't have a choice.

"Because I can." I fill a canister with water from the pitcher on the counter and grab a pocket knife out of a drawer. I doubt I'll need it. The island is divided. Half mine. Half his. A bargain we set in stone no one would dare cross, but the living are unpredictable. Even more so after they've died.

I slam the drawer shut and grab my water bottle. I can't be here and look at her any longer. Not when she reeks of Cass. His scent oozes out of her pores. Subtle at first, but the longer she and I are together, the stronger it becomes.

He's marked her as his.

I wrinkle my nose as I walk past. "You smell. Take a shower before I get back."

"You're leaving?" The sorrow in Wednesday's tone catches me off guard.

I stop at the door, my hand on the nob. Deja vu hits me hard. If I'm not careful, Wednesday and I will make the same mistakes over. I refuse to let history repeat itself.

"Don't pretend you want me around, Darling." Hate me, I remind myself. She needs to hate me, even if making her do so cuts my heart out. "Besides, I have things to do."

"But I just got here. You said we needed to talk."

"That was last night." When I thought about taking Wednesday home and protecting her from afar. I was reckless in bringing her to Neverland. I'd forgotten how quickly emotions can cloud judgment which is why I don't hold it against Wednesday that she left with Cass. I backed her into a corner and she reacted. Doesn't mean I like her decisions. "You made your choice."

"What choice, Peter? What are you talking about?"

Something new burns inside me. A fire I'm unfamiliar with climbs my neck. I clench my fists. An overwhelming need to punch something sinks its teeth in me. I vaguely recognize the sensation. It's similar to the feeling I got when her sister, Tyle, was around. Only worse. "I'll be back later."

"What am I supposed to do?"

Not sleep with the first man you find on the island!

"I don't know. Figure it out. You seem to be more than capable of entertaining yourself," I say and slam the door behind me.

CHAPTER 15
Peter

I smell him even after I leave the treehouse.

Cass's scent sears my nostrils. It wafts through the trees, carrying in the breeze. It surrounds me, poking the fury beneath my skin. I told him to be her friend, not her fuck toy. I wanted him to charm Wednesday and win her heart, not stick his crooked dick where it doesn't belong.

I shout, anger consuming my thoughts. I swing at the tree nearest me. My knuckles ache as the trunk cracks, but I feel better.

Until I smell it again.

Cass's fae mark.

My feet take me to the beach while my mind pelts me with images of what they've done. Memories of Wendy and James merge with the present. Hundreds of living years have passed, and the sting is still just as sharp.

"Hey, Pete. Can we—"

The world fades to black. A high pitch ring fills my ears. I lose myself and have no idea what I'm doing.

When I can see again, both of my hands are around Cass's neck. Xyris and Emmit pull me off. I shake free of their grips and hold my hands up. I'm good. I won't do it again.

Cass coughs. He rubs the red skin, the sight of my mark on him is satisfying. "What the hell, Peter?"

"You slept with her?" I yell. That feeling climbs my neck again. I want to strangle him, snuff his stupid faery life out with my bare hands just so he can never touch her again. I take a deep breath and test every bit of restraint I have. Cass is my friend, I remind myself. Not my enemy.

"I did what you told me to do."

"I told you to be her friend. Not fuck her, Cass." I run my hands through my hair and pull at the roots. His smell is everywhere. In the air. On the sand. On my skin. I run to the water and stick my hands in a wave. I need to get it off before I puke.

"She told me to man up or she'd find someone else. Who did you think she'd wind up with? You?" He waits for me to answer, but I don't. He's right. Wednesday would rather peel her skin off than climb in bed with me last night.

"But you marked her." Like a fucking territorial cat in heat.

"Where's your shadow, Peter?" he asks, changing the topic.

I glare, despite the validity of his question. His presence would explain what I'm feeling, but he's gone, roaming the island. I could always sense his emotions, but they've never felt like my own. He is not angry with Cass. This is all me. "We both know I have no control over where my shadow self goes or what he does."

"You haven't been this pissed off in years. Not since he left you."

Cass is right. I'm feeling things. I drop my shoulders at the realization and a new emotion pushes through. Shame. "Is it just me? Or does anyone else feel different?"

"I cried this morning," Scarlet whispers. Heidi puts her arms around her lover's shoulders. "I woke up and let out all the pain I'd been holding in. It poured out of me. I couldn't stop until every last tear was shed."

"And I felt bad for her," Heidi adds. "I wanted to take her sorrow away, but I was so happy she felt something more than fear. That's when I realized I wasn't angry anymore."

"The island is shifting, Peter." Emmit looks at Cass. They talk amongst each other, in a silent language only they understand. Belle taught me how to hear it once. I couldn't understand a word she said, but it sounded like tinkling bells.

"Why are we pretending you're the bad guy?" Aria asks. "What don't we know?"

"Everything." I look at Cass and Emmit. They nod simultaneously. I don't need to hear their words to know what they are saying. It's time everyone knew how they came to the island and what Wednesday means for their future.

73

CHAPTER 16
Wednesday

N othing.

There is absolutely nothing useful in this damned treehouse.

The moment Peter left I began searching for something. Anything to use against him or to give me leverage, but I've come up with jack shit. Peter's room is painfully bare. His dresser holds a handful of white shirts, green or khaki shorts, and a few pairs of jeans. All of which are lying on his bedroom floor.

I don't care.

He's made a mess of my life.

I can make a mess in his house.

Peter's bathroom mirrors Cass's, with a large banana leaf shower and a toilet and sink. I try not to think about how the basics of life, like plumbing, work in Neverland. It's not likely there's a septic tank in this tree and I don't want to know where all the nastiness goes.

I walk back into the hallway and set my hands on my hips. All that's left is my room and the open living space. I doubt the books on his shelf hold any secrets. Judging by the layer of dust on the covers, I don't think he's touched them in a while.

That leaves the kitchen—if the space can even be called that—and about a dozen cabinets and drawers. The whole wall across from the living room is storage. Not abnormal, except every other aspect that makes a kitchen habitable is missing. The stove. The sink. Hell, there isn't even a refrigerator. My stomach growls, but any hope I had of finding something to eat has died.

I start tearing through the cabinets on one end of the wall and make my way down the line. Everything comes out. Blankets, sheets, and pillowcases on the bottom. All a crisp, bleached white. There's a knitted throw blanket in the cabinet next to that, along with an old crusty bear. Tufts of fur linger on my fingers as I turn it over. There's a patch on the backside void of fur. I smile; a distant memory I can't place settles into my bones, like a warm cup of coffee.

I place the bear back on the blanket and tuck it in for safekeeping. Tossing it across the room and onto the floor feels wrong.

The next cabinet is boring. Big bowls for mixing and a few other odds and ends. The same can be said for all the other cabinets. I continue to pull everything out, on principle. Every little inconvenience I can cause Peter is a win in my book.

It's not until I reach the top corner of the last cabinet I search that I find something... peculiar.

My fingers skim across the hardcover of a book. I pull it off the shelf and hop off the counter back onto the floor. Short people problems. My five-foot-five stature makes me full of fun, but vertically challenged most days.

The lettering on the cover and spine is worn. Faded with years of age and devoured by dust. The hard backing separates from the binding as I open it. My soul screams as the book cracks. It's a first edition publication of Peter and Wendy by J. M. Barrie.

I flip through the pages, carefully turning each one. They're as delicate as the petals of a wilted rose. The last thing I want is for one to tear or separate from the binding. I don't give two shits if the damage would upset Peter. Hurting a book this old ravages my feeble teacher heart.

I take it to the wingback chair and cross my legs as I settle onto the cushions. I've read this book a thousand times over. Watched the movies, and the one with Jeremy Sumpter is my favorite. Read about a dozen retellings. But nothing has come close to the feeling of holding a first edition print.

All children grow up, except one.

It dawns on me, as I re-read the ancient pages, that there are bits of truth in the tale, but most of it is wrong. Peter did grow up and his lost boys aren't a band of children, but a dozen or so wayward misfits, most of which he ignores. I frown as I take in the story, pillaging through each line as if it were the first time I've read it. Taking apart each sentence and comparing it to what little I've learned about Neverland in the last twenty-four hours... which isn't much.

"You shouldn't be reading that."

Cass's voice makes me jump. I slam the book shut. A cloud of dust plumes, blooming in the air and tickles my nose until I sneeze, once. Twice. After the third time, my eyes are itchy and my nose is runny.

Cass picks a handkerchief from the pile of linens on the floor and hands it to me. "You good?"

"Yeah." I wipe my eyes and then blow my nose. "Dust allergy. What are you doing here?"

His lips lift into a lopsided smile that makes my stomach flip. He tucks his hands into the pockets of his khaki shorts and shrugs. "Can't a guy miss his girl?"

"You're such a sap." I roll my eyes but I know he can see the blush on my cheeks.

I don't know how long I've been sitting here. A couple of hours. Maybe? Time is irrelevant when the sky is various shades of pink, orange and blue. What I do know is we haven't been apart long enough for Cass to actually miss me.

"If you're catching feelings for me, we need to quit now before things get crazy."

"Life in Neverland is madness, Wens." Cass sits in the seat beside me, a gray accent chair with a lower back and deflated tufts of fabric. "Now that you're here, it'll soon come to an end."

"Does anyone on the island understand you?" I laugh because I have no idea what he just said. It's either a whacked compliment or a threat wrapped in velvet.

"Feel like running away with me?"

"I'm thinking no is the safe answer." The last time I played a game like that, Peter's brought me to a beautiful island I can't enjoy because there's no return ticket home. I don't think these people know what sarcasm is, and it would be my luck Cass would have a one-way ticket to the River Styx. "Although, I might change my mind if you can sneak me back home."

Cass reaches forward, brushing his finger against my cheek, and tucks my hair behind my ears. "Your soul burns too bright for the world you were born into."

"I'll take that as a no?"

He shakes his head. Beads of water drip off his blonde hair. I can't help but wonder if he went swimming before coming to see me, or if he's just sweaty from the island heat.

My mind strays to what Cass could have been doing. Chopping wood shirtless. Playing ball in the sand. Doing pull-ups on a tree branch, toning his already taught muscles. My frustrations with Peter turned me on. That man gets under my skin in the most aggravating of ways and sweet Cass is going to get the benefit.

"We're going to the mirror pool." Cass's voice seeps into my lust-filled thoughts. I lick my lips. His eyes follow the movement, watching me with the same desire I'm fighting. "I thought you might want to join us."

"Who is we?" There's one person on this island I'd rather not see, especially if water is involved. I would rather Peter come home to an empty house and trip over the mess, forcing him to deal with it all on his own. I want him pissed off that I messed with his things. I want him wondering if I'm off with Cass. And I want him cursing my name, and wishing he'd never brought me to Neverland.

"Not Peter," Cass answers. It must be obvious that I don't like that man because his lips lift into a delicious smirk.

"Okay. Give me a minute to get ready." I want to hide the book from Peter and read some more of it later. Based on Cass's warning not to talk about the tale, I have a feeling it was hidden from Peter. Not by him.

I step over the obstacle course that is Peter's possessions and head to my room. As soon as I'm through the door I spot my suitcase, a rolling leopard print travel bag, on my bed.

It's a unique pattern. Neon blue is the primary color with black spots. I bought it to piss off Tyle when we were eighteen. It's a one-of-a-kind she had her heart set on. I hate the damn thing. It's too flashy but its uniqueness makes it easy to find in an airport.

Or a mythical island.

I hide Peter's book in the top drawer of my dresser and then walk to my bed. I unzip my case. Everything from the bachelorette party is still there. My toothbrush. Clothes. eReader. I pull each item out and set it on the bed. My heart squeezes with homesickness. Never in a million years did I think I'd want to return to take-out, Netflix, and the simplicity of my life, but I miss every boring, predictable aspect of it.

Cass's knuckles rasp against the doorframe. "You okay?"

I look over at him, my eReader clutched to my chest, tears in my eyes because its battery is full. When I held it last, it was on its last leg, a mere fifteen percent. Someone charged it for me.

"He went back," I whisper.

"What are you talking about?"

I look at all of my things. Tears fall down my cheeks. I think this is what Peter wanted to tell me last night, that he was going back, that he might have taken me, and I stupidly pushed him away because I was drunk and pissed off. I ruined my chances of going home.

I'm so mad at myself I could scream, but I'm even angrier with Peter. How could he just let me leave? Why didn't he speak up? If he would have said something, I wouldn't be here.

I hate him.

I hate him so much it hurts.

"Peter went back to Florida without me." I squeeze my eyes shut, desperately trying to stop the flow of tears before they get out of control. "He lied."

"Babe." Warm arms wrap around me.

I bury my face in Cass's chest. It's not often I feel completely helpless. There's always a way out. A next step that changes everything. A bright side. I'm having a hard time finding the silver lining today. I think I've done well to keep level-headed, but this feels like rock bottom.

I need to get home.

After a few shaky breaths, I realize I need to stop pushing Cass away. This is what I wanted yesterday. Him under a love-drunk spell. I want him so wrapped up in me his lips loosen. I need him to spill the island's secrets. I don't believe we're in Neverland. Sure that may be what they call this place, but it doesn't exist. As for the weird sun anomaly... I have an answer for that too.

Alaska.

Alaska has what's called a polar night. The sun hides from one region for almost sixty days, casting them in darkness. Wherever we are, it must be a fluke area of the world like that. I'll search for the name of this island's phenomena, whenever I find cell service again.

As my breaths begin to steady, I notice something odd about my beautiful jailer. I raise my head to look Cass in the eyes. "Can I ask you a question?"

He smiles down at me, perfectly straight teeth bared. "Anything."

"Why can't I hear your heartbeat?"

CHAPTER 17
Wednesday

Dying *is the greatest adventure of them all.* Peter's words echo in my mind. *Death is unpredictable. Sometimes people come back... different.*

I pull back and place my hand over my chest, searching for my own heartbeat. It thrashes in my chest, thumping with enough vigor to keep both myself and Cass alive. Each thrum beneath my skin should be steadying, but it only creates more worry. More uncertainty in the line of understanding I've only just crossed.

"I see you've found one of our secrets." Cass's smile falls. He walks to the edge of the bed and sits, disregarding the clothes that cover the mattress. "I was hoping to have more time with you before you realized our truths."

"What truths?" I push my suitcase to the headboard and sit beside him. My shirts wrinkle underneath my weight and my shoes topple off the edge. Cass takes my hand in his. I notice the warmth coming off his skin. Something impossibly unnatural for someone without a pulse.

"Neverland is an..." He pauses. His bushy brows push together while trying to find the right words. "An in between place. A place where nothing lives or dies."

"That's impossible." Neverland doesn't exist. This is Alaska. A beautiful, mysterious place where the laws of life are sometimes bent. Not broken. Existence after death, an in-between after the soul has left the body, that kind of madness doesn't exist.

"Is it?" Cass takes my hand and places it over where his heart should be. There is no drum of life. No rise and fall of his chest. We stay like that for minutes, longer than any person could dare to hold their breath. Even without the steady rhythm of breathing, the heart should be doing something, getting angry at the lack of oxygen, yelling at the lungs with its fists. My hand never moves, not once. "Everyone on this island is stuck, Wednesday, somewhere between life and death."

"So this is purgatory?" My heart beats, I remind myself. It beats, which means I'm alive.

Cass's doesn't.

What does that make him? *No, stop thinking like that, Wednesday.* Cass is lying. He has to be. Oh, god. My thoughts flip, jumping tracks like a train out of control.

Did I sleep with a dead guy?

Am I a necrophile?

"I see your mind spinning." He chuckles, and the sound makes me angry. Nothing about what he's telling me is funny. I slept with a corpse last night!

"I'm as alive as you are," he adds, answering my unspoken question. "My body needs food. My lungs need air. Just because my heart doesn't beat doesn't mean I can't feel, Wednesday."

Feeling was never my concern. "Can you die?"

"Yes, but not of old age."

Cass pulls a small knife from his pocket. The blade flips open with the push of a button. He presses the tip to the palm of his hand. Bright red blood seeps out of the small hole, proving that he can be hurt.

He pulls the blade away and holds his hand up. A bead of blood trails down his arm. By the time it drips off of his elbow and onto the sheet, the cut has healed.

"I can bleed and bruise, but it's incredibly hard to kill me. Not impossible, I've watched my kind die more times than I'd like, but not an easy task."

I take Cass's hand and run my finger over the spot where the cut was. His skin is impossibly smooth, the hole sealed from the inside out in seconds.

Seeing is believing.

I wish I had closed my eyes. "Is everyone on the island like you?"

"No." He cradles my cheek in his hand and forces me to look up at him as he speaks. "Emmit is the same as me. Aria, Xyris, Scarlett, and the rest of The Lost are souls who veered off track on the way to their next life. Unclaimed by the underworld. Forgotten by their own. They are forever stuck, forced to only experience their last emotion."

"That sounds horrible."

He nods. "Heidi and Scarlett were murdered by Heidi's stepdad because he was closed minded. The bastard forced her to watch as he tortured Scar. She died in fear, hoping that Heidi could save her. Heidi died fighting."

"That's awful." I think back to when Peter pushed me off the boat. To the fear of missing out on my life. To the pain and pressure on my lungs and body. I wouldn't want to stay like that for all eternity. Not if there was another choice.

He nods. "They're stuck in those feelings, reliving the last moments of their lives. So long as they're here, they'll never find peace."

"And here I thought she didn't like me," I mumble aloud.

Cass chuckles but the sound is forced. He's trying to keep his light-hearted, carefree attitude, but I can see how hard it is for him to talk about this. "Trust me, beautiful. You'll know if Heidi doesn't like you."

"So...is Peter?" I swallow hard, not wanting to ask the question. This is a lot to take in and I'm not sure how much more I can swallow.

"He's not one of The Lost, but he's not like Emmit and me either." Cass sighs and scratches the back of his head. "He's...a devotion gone wrong."

I nod, not understanding, but I don't push for more. Cass is as white as a ghost. The golden glow of his skin is gone, muted by the harshness of his truths. It must have been hard to tell me as much as he did.

I lean over and cup the back of his neck, pulling his lips to mine. I kiss him, more for my benefit than his. I'm relieved to feel the flutter of lust pool in my stomach.

Cass breaks our kiss but stays close, his lips a whisper away. "You don't have to pretend, Wednesday. I understand if you don't want to do this anymore."

"This changes nothing. You and I..." My breath hitches. I can't lie and say that we're something because while I like Cass, there's someone else standing in the way. "We're having fun."

Cass slides his hand under my shirt and kisses me again. His fingers play with my nipple. It puckers, tightening because of his touch.

I fall back onto the bed, my suitcase annoyingly in the way. I push it to the ground as Cass tugs at my shorts and panties. They slide to my ankles and I kick them off. He doesn't try to drag out my pleasure this time. Instead, he's quick to free himself and find my entrance.

I don't ask for a condom. We've done it once without so there is no point. This time though I tell him, "I don't want a repeat of last time. If you come inside me again, we're done."

"Yes, my shining star," he says, pushing into me.

I squeeze my eyes shut and breathe through the discomfort. I'm sore from yesterday and skipping foreplay has my walls pretty dry, but with each thrust of his hips things feel better. I push on his shoulders, wanting a new position, but Cass pins my wrists to the mattress. He tunnels into me, his thrusts rough and claiming.

Last night I wanted to be punished, but today I just want to feel good. My mind hasn't let go of our conversation or that I could have gone home. It's hard to enjoy the ride. I fake an orgasm to keep Cass's ego from deflating. That seems to be what he was waiting for because a few minutes later he's pulling out and finishing on one of my shirts.

I lay there and stare up at the ceiling. *He has no heartbeat. He should be dead. I fucked a dead guy... again.*

Cass turns onto his side. He rests his cheek against his fist, hazel eyes looking at me. "Has anyone told you how beautiful you are after sex? Your skin glows with life."

I exhale a laugh, unsure of how else to respond. "I don't think I'll ever get used to how you talk."

"Good." He smiles and if I wasn't already struggling to catch my breath I would be breathless because this is the type of smile to suck the air from your lungs. "That means I will forever have you in the palm of my hand."

"Easy, killer. I wouldn't go that far." I let Cass thread his fingers with mine. I can't get over how warm his skin is. Without a heartbeat, there is no circulation. What's giving him life if not that? "I like the way you make me feel. That's it. Don't make this more than it is."

Cass rolls on top of me. His legs spread until he's sitting on my lap. He leans over, one hand on either side of my shoulders, and says, "I like that you make me feel, Wednesday. You have no idea how long it's been since I've thought about anything but..." He cuts himself of and presses a quick kiss to my lips. "We need to get dressed."

"Oh? Do we?"

"Yup." Cass climbs off of me and reaches for his shorts. "You're coming with me to the mirror pool. There's something I want to show you."

CHAPTER 18
Wednesday

The grass is soft under my legs. Not itchy or wet. I changed out of Tyle's bikini and into my cutout one piece. It's black with a thin strip of fabric connecting the top to the bottoms. It's basically another two-piece but this one is clean which makes my lady bits happy. I also put on a pair of shorts Cass and I found at the Pirate's Market and paired it with the *ACOTAR* shirt I used as a pajama in the Keys.

I sit on a small knoll that overlooks an open field. Cass, Xyris, and Heidi run around under the cotton candy sky. The sun has shifted, coloring the clouds in deep hues of purple and blue. This is the closest they get to nightfall. Not as bright, but never fully dark.

Scarlett sets a mason jar filled with lightning bugs beside me. Their butts glow bright and then the light winks out for a heartbeat before lighting again.

"Catching them is half the fun," she whispers, her lips lifting into a small smile.

"If it creeps or crawls it's not for me," I admit.

I've never liked bugs. As a kid, they gave me nightmares. The only creatures I could stand were butterflies and dragonflies. Eventually, I learned not to scream when a bee flew past me, but it took a lot of willpower. Looking at the lightning bugs, I know they are harmless, but that doesn't stop the urge to run away from making a quick appearance.

"I don't like them either." Scarlet stares at the little jar of bugs. The lid has small, oblong holes in it that look like they were made by the point of a knife. "The lightning bugs." She's quiet, always so hard to hear. I have to strain my ears to catch what she says even though the world around us is still. "Their glow flickers on and off. It makes me feel... bad."

I think back to my conversation with Cass. Forever in a state of fear. I understand now why she never speaks above a whisper. The fear of being heard by the wrong person, being caught and tortured again for simply existing and loving someone must always be on her mind. My thoughts wander to what memories the flickering light of the firefly's butt might trigger. I shudder, too many horror movie scenes coming to mind. "Then why come?"

Scar's lips lift slightly. Her amber gaze follows Heidi as her partner struggles to catch fireflies without killing them. "Because it makes her happy."

Heidi grunts and curses under her breath. She peeks between her fingers, her brows knit, and she curses again. She jumps in the air and clasps her palms together, repeating her failing attempts to fill her jar.

I look at Scarlett skeptically. "That's happy?"

"Yeah." She laughs. The sound is breathy and light. It's barely louder than the whispers I've grown used to, but the sound makes me feel joy. Somewhere beneath all the worry and constant torture of living, Scarlett has happiness. I don't know how long it lasts, but knowing that she isn't solely stuck in a state of fear like Cass described is a relief. "Heidi's got a resting bitch face, but she means well."

"If you say so."

Silence falls between us. At first, it's nothing more than quiet air, but the longer we sit, the thicker it becomes. I'm sure the tension is in my mind. Scarlett is busy watching her mate grunt and growl while I watch Cass. He effortlessly fills two jars with glowing bugs, laughing and joking with Emmit and Xyris between handfuls.

There's a heaviness in my chest. Questions that burn under my skin, dying to be asked. But how? Where do I even start without raising suspicions? "Have you guys been together long?"

"Long enough to feel like forever, but I love her." Scarlett pulls her knees in and hugs her legs. She rests her chin on her knees. "Even when all I want to do is flee."

"I might be overstepping, but that doesn't sound like love."

"I don't expect you to understand. You haven't been around long enough." She meets my gaze. "I like you, Wednesday, but I hope you never find out what I mean."

"You've been here a long time, though. Haven't you?" I hold my breath and hope Scarlett doesn't dig too deep. Heidi would question me and want to know why I'm asking. She's always on edge, understandably. I can't imagine growing up in a world with so much hate she was murdered for falling in love.

Scarlet sighs. She plucks a blade of grass out of the ground and tears it into tiny pieces. "It feels that way, but I'm not sure. Time isn't linear here. It just...is."

Cass comes over with two glowing jars in his hands. His smile is wide, eyes alight with life. "Are you ladies ready?"

"I still say she needed to catch the damn bugs herself," Heidi growls, her eyes narrowed into slits on me.

"Shut it, Heidi." Xyris spits. "Em caught damn near all your lightning bugs. You'd still be out there, killing each one you touch if it wasn't for him."

"Whatever." She rolls her eyes.

I stand and brush the dirt off my ass. Cass leans forward and wraps his arm around my waist. He leans in, nuzzling his nose against my neck. It tickles and a laugh leaves my lips. I smile against his skin, relieved my mind isn't stuck on the lack of heartbeat problem. It's hard to make a man want to spill his secrets if touching him makes me want to puke.

"Ugh. Get a room."

"You're just jealous." Cass steps back and drapes an arm over my shoulders.

"Please. I wouldn't touch your sloppy seconds with a ten-foot pole."

A small part of me jumps for joy. They heard our bedroom romp last night, or about it. News is traveling which means if it hasn't already reached Peter's ears, it will.

Before I can open my mouth to spit a rebuttal, Xyris takes me by the elbow and pulls me out of Cass's embrace.

Cass lets me go, freely, and I slam into Xyris's hard chest. Xyris looks down at me. His eyes are the color of an auburn sun, red, and orange, and brown. I've come to realize that everyone here has unique irises, and I wonder if their color has to do with their deaths because no living person has eyes as vibrant.

"Don't let Heidi get under your skin." Xyris reaches up and tucks my hair behind my ears, using both hands. "There is nothing sloppy about you."

"I don't need you sticking up for me." I step back and clear my throat. "But thanks."

"What did I tell you?" Cass chuckles. "Fucker is always trying to steal my girl."

"I thought you and Emmit were together." My cheeks heat, embarrassed to have to ask.

"Oh, I'm one hundred and ten percent his." Xyris looks at Emmit and winks. "But we like to add a little spice every now and then. Don't we, baby?"

Emmit shrugs. "When you've been together as long as we have, adding something new from time to time keeps the spark alive."

"And you're okay with this?" I look at Cass. For someone who calls me a shining star, and constantly tells me how amazing I am, he doesn't seem bothered by the idea of Xyris trying to sleep with me.

He shrugs. "Who am I to stop you?"

The man who had his dick in me a few hours ago! My jaw drops in disbelief.

"Baby, just because I fucked you doesn't mean you can't explore everything this island has to offer," he says, almost as if he can hear my unspoken thought.

I don't know what to say. I think I'm in shock.

Cass cups my cheeks. He presses his forehead to mine until he's all I see. "If you want to bring someone else into the bedroom with us, I'll welcome them. If you want to shack up with Captain Fucks Everything Up too, go for it. I'm not going to punish you for wanting to feel everything Neverland has to offer because feeling is a gift. Live in the now and enjoy what this life has to offer."

"Does the same go for you?" I feel guilty asking. I'm using him but that doesn't mean I want to catch a disease. If Neverland doesn't have electricity I doubt it has antibiotics.

"No. You're the first partner I've had in years. There is no one on this island I want besides you."

"Get a room," Heidi coughs.

"Come on now, Heidi. Don't be a prude." Xyris elbows her in the side. "We all know how much you love voyeurism."

She flips him off and links arms with Scarlet. They walk across the grassy knoll, paying no mind to the boys and me.

Emmit looks up at the sky. Faint traces of stars permeate through the clouds. Their light is stuck behind the tufts, permanently lost to us. "We need to go."

"Go where?" I ask.

Cass hands me the jar of glowing bugs. "To the best kept secret in all of Neverland."

CHAPTER 19
Wednesday

"**N**o. Absolutely not."

I stand at the mouth of a cave on the side of a mountain they call Neverpeek. Jagged rocks lay on top of each other, forming a makeshift opening I'm supposed to blindly walk into.

"You're going to miss the best part." Cass has been waiting for me to build up the courage and follow the others inside but I can't force my legs to move. A cold sweat has covered my skin to the point that thinking about stepping inside the mountain makes me physically sick.

"I'm sure it's cool, but I don't know, Cass." I press my back against the stone. Crisp dew permeates through my shirt and grounds my body.

"Trust me," he insists, running his fingers down my arms. I'm sure he's trying to be comforting but his touch undoes the dew's magic and makes my skin clammy.

My heart races, the palpitations alarmingly fast, then slow, then fast again. "You're asking a lot for a guy I just met."

"Wednesday, can you honestly tell me we feel like strangers?" Cass ducks to meet my gaze even though I'm trying not to look at him. "Can you say without a shadow of a doubt that you don't feel it in your bones, the way I do. This thing between us is stronger than first-time-fuck-lust." He arches his eyebrows. "If that's all you feel we are, I'll hike down to the beach with you and chill there for the rest of the day." He takes my hands and squeezes them. "But if you feel even an inkling more, I'm asking you to take the leap and trust me."

I can't deny there's a sense of familiarity when Cass and I are together. Being with him has the same comforting feeling of walking into my house with a pecan pie candle burning, an ease that hugs us like an easy blanket. He doesn't feel new. He feels old, in the weirdest, most amazing sense of the word.

I glance at the mouth of the cave and notice the downhill incline, new worries creeping in. "What happens if it rains? "

My question is met with a flash of teeth. "It never rains in Neverland."

I swallow hard and nod. Of course it doesn't. That would require the sky to change and it's always the most annoyingly beautiful shade of pink.

There's a persistent throb behind my left eye but I step onto the first gray stone. It's wider than me and if I were to lie across it would be nearly twice as long. My legs shake, but I force them to take another step and another.

Cass skips ahead and crouches low in front of me. He twists when I get close. His eyes, the same shade as the evergreens that surround us, shine. "Want a lift?"

"Am I that pathetic?" I don't protest. I trust that he knows every foothold and low lying arch of this cave. I'd be stupid not to climb onto his back. It's funny though, the first time we did this feels like a lifetime ago. *How was it just yesterday?*

Cass hums, drawing out the inevitable truth of how painfully unprepared my life has made me.

Did I expect to be stolen away to an island full of gorgeous men?

No. I don't think even the best read novel could have made me ready for this, but I do wish I had gone hiking at least once before today because I am exhausted. My hands are swollen and tingling and we haven't done anything but walk.

"You are beautifully innocent." Cass turns his head and kisses the side of my arm. "I prefer you this way. It means I get to play hero for a little bit."

"As opposed to what? Being the villain?" I'm joking, but something stirs in my chest. It's a precarious sensation.

Cass chuckles, avoiding the question. We hike deeper into the cave. The stones are slippery and uneven, but as suspected he knows when to reach out and steady himself. He turns a corner and the little light carrying in from the opening disappears. If not for the glow of the bugs, we'd be walking in darkness.

"Was this your plan all along?" I ask, the hackles on the back of my neck standing on edge. The further we trek, the more I regret not trusting my instincts. I can't shake this feeling of unease. "To earn my trust so you can kill me later?"

"Telling you my plan would ruin the surprise."

Cass sets me down and I slip. My converse were made for sidewalks and basketball courts, not island adventures. He grabs my waist and steadies me. I look over my shoulder and flash a thank you smile.

"Are you sure you're ready for me to spoil my devious plan?" He arches one eyebrow and gives me a smolder that would make Flynn Rider jealous. "Fine," he says in a mocking, pubescent tone. "You're right. I need you to die. But the question is how?"

He rubs his chin and twists invisible beard hair. I stare at him, completely lost for words and the insane fucker winks. I laugh because it's the only thing I know how to do. For a second, I was worried. I almost believed him.

"You're crazy, you know that."

"I've heard it a time or two." Cass tucks his hands into the pockets of his shorts, a cheeky grin on display. We walk, side by side, on (thankfully) level ground, the only sound in the cave our footsteps and beating hearts.

"Hey, Wednesday?" he says, his voice a whisper in the near darkness.

"Hmm?"

"Look up."

Stalactites hang from the roof like teeth reaching down to eat us. It would be terrifying if not for the glow of green and yellow algae decorating each spike like an inverted Christmas tree.

Cass takes his mason jar and twists the lid. His lightning bugs fly free. My first reaction is to recoil and hide, but as I watch them drift up toward the glow, they remind me of the night sky. I stare at them, in awe of their beauty.

"Open your jar." He nudges me with his elbow.

I twist my lid free, releasing another slow swarm of twinkling lights.

"I haven't seen stars in almost two hundred years." There's a longing in his voice. "This is the next best thing."

My heart squeezes. I've only been in Neverland for one night and already miss the little comforts. I hadn't thought about the big things, like how I'll never get a full night's rest because there will always be light. I'll never make another wish on the first star because there aren't any. How many more little things am I missing that I haven't even realized? What did Cass lose when he became trapped here?

"It's amazing." I watch the bugs light's flicker on and off, with no rhyme or reason, as they fly higher in the cave. It's easy to imagine them as stars in the sky. I connect the dots, creating my own little dipper and north star.

"Where is everyone else?"

"A little further down. There's a pool of water if you're interested in swimming."

A chill covers me. I'm not ready to face the water again. "Do you think we could hang out here for a bit? I'm not in the mood for a swim."

"Of course." Cass kisses the side of my head.

We sit in the dirt and lean our backs against a large stone, creating our own constellations and talking about make-believe worlds with monsters, magic, and a lost princess that could save them all.

CHAPTER 20
Wednesday

"**I** see you found your things," Peter snarls when I walk through the door. He's sitting in the corner, an ancient copy of *Pride and Prejudice* in his hands. "Wonder how they got here?"

"I don't know. Crazy how things just show up in this house. Like the mess on the floor." I smirk at the blankets, pots, and knickknacks everywhere. "Didn't feel like cleaning it up?"

Peter closes his book, eyes narrowed on me. "Have fun with your boyfriend today?"

"Cass isn't my boyfriend."

"I can smell him on you."

"Sucks for you." I run my fingers down my stomach and sink them into the hand of my shorts while grabbing my chest with the other hand. "Could have been your name I was screaming in the woods."

I lick the finger that I tucked into my panties. There's nothing there but Peter's eyes flare at the sight. I've never seen a man get worked up over me. The power of knowing I can make him squirm is intoxicating. "Too bad you fucked it up."

Peter is up and out of the chair faster than my brain can follow. His hand touches my shoulder. He pushes me until my back hits the wall. "Careful, Darling. Keep it up and I'll be fighting fire with fire."

"You can try, but I've got to want you for it to work, Peter, and I'd fuck every man on his island before touching you. You repulse me."

He chuckles. "Your nipples disagree."

He pinches one and I nearly come from his touch. I slap him because I hate how much I want him. He takes it like my hand is nothing more than the breeze caressing his skin.

He brushes his nose against my cheek. "Naughty girls get punished,

94

Darling. Are you a naughty girl?" he asks, darkness filling the blue of his irises.

"What are you?" I wonder, not meaning to ask the question aloud.

Peter's lips lift into a wicked smirk. "You think your boyfriend told you everything about Neverland? You're wrong."

Squirm and stand taller. "I know enough."

"Do you?" He unsheathes a knife from the holster at his side. The hand on my shoulder turns and his forearm pushes against my neck. The pressure teeters between thrilling and uncomfortable, but it's the look in his eyes that scares me. The sheer hatred burning through a lusty haze.

"Peter, you're hurting me."

"Did your precious boyfriend tell you how time works?" He runs the blunt edge of the blade down my cheek.

The metal is cold, but that's not why I shiver. "We're in between life and death, day and night."

He cuts my shirt open, slicing the printed mountain in half, then snaps the string holding my bathing suit top up. It falls, leaving me bare before him. Peter takes in the swell of my breasts with his eyes. The hunger in them matches the need ripping through me.

Peter holds the knife in his fingers and presses his palm against my chest. "Your heart is racing,"

I take a slow breath, noticing his pupils constrict. The truth that I want him as much if not more than he wants me is an anchor. It keeps me in this moment, lets me feel the ache inside, instead of remembering that I'm supposed to be a tease, making his life miserable.

"Do you know why you feel so much, Darling? It's because your precious human heart is trying to keep pace with the world you live in while existing in mine." He pulls away and slashes the blade across my arm.

"Asshole!" I cover my wound with my hand. Fury rips through any heady thoughts I had. Tears pool in my eyes, stinging almost as bad as my arm. "You cut me!"

"Did I?" He smirks, and I don't know how I ever found him attractive.

"What do you mean, *did I*?" I show him the wound on my arm but

95

it's gone, the only indication that I was hurt is the blood on my hand and a barely visible scar. "I... how?"

Peter leans against the counter, stepping on the blankets I threw on the floor. "How long would you say it takes a cut like that to heal?"

"I don't know... maybe a few minutes of pressure for the bleeding to stop and a few days for the scab to be gone."

"Very good, Darling. How long did it take here?"

"Seconds," I whisper.

"A second in our world is a minute in yours. Minutes, hours. Hours, days. You can't trust time." He taps his temple. "It will fuck with your mind, your emotions. Neverland will twist everything you know about the world, your life, and turn it on its side."

I feel the blood drain from my face. Have I been gone for weeks? Months? At this point, if I was to find a way home, would I even have a home to go back to or would all of my things be sold, my apartment re-rented?

"The only place on the island you're safe is in this tree house. Hate me, if you will, but the Island's magic can't touch you here. Your feelings are real, your thoughts safe. Out there." He points at the door. "You're powerless against it."

"I don't believe you."

"Why? Because you like Cass? That's cute. He's not who you think he is. None of them are." He tucks his knife back into its holster and pushes off the counter. He heads to the door, ready to leave me alone in this house. Again.

"What does that make you, Peter?" I yell, venom biting every word.

His steps falter. He stands in the middle of the room, shoulders rolled forward. His breaths are slow, controlled to the point they're rhythmical. He doesn't look at me but I feel the weight of every word as he says, "I'm what you made me be."

CHAPTER 21
Wednesday

Peter was right.

Time isn't linear.

I thought I had figured out day versus night—the sky brighter blue versus the deep purple wisps that appear later in the day —but not nearly enough time passes in between for it to be the equivalent of the sun falling and moon rising. The only thing I've consistently counted is the times I've fallen asleep, eight so far, and even that is unreliable. I can't tell the difference between a nap and a night's rest.

The longer I'm on the island, the more I question.

How did The Lost come to Neverland?

Why can't they leave?

What happened to Peter? He never flies or crows like the stories describe. Has he lost his spirit? His magic? Where did it all come from in the first place?

Cass is no help. He dodges my questions with kisses and sex. If he wasn't so good in bed I might be mad, but watching Peter's face burn red whenever we pass makes me care less and less about the unanswered. I'll eventually find what I'm searching for.

One way or another.

But I can't ask Peter anything because he's keeping his distance, which only pisses me off and gives me even more questions. Why bring me to this stupid island if the plan was to ignore me? He made me feel like the only girl in the world when we were in Florida. He set my soul on fire, woke every nerve in my body, just to douse it all in ice water.

Because here I'm nothing.

I can't make sense of it.

And since Cass refuses to let me stay over anymore, I'm forced to sleep under Peter's roof every night, in the bed I woke up on my first night here even though the treehouse is always empty.

Peter makes it a point not to be present when I am. Perhaps his absence is a token of truce. If he spends every evening the way he is tonight, tangled up in Aria's lips, I'm glad he's not around.

Heat climbs my neck as I watch him share a glass of whiskey with her on the other side of the bonfire. Aria takes his crystal tumbler and looks up at him through long lashes. Her lips taste his against the glass.

Peter leans close, whispering into her ear. I remember what his warm breath against my skin felt like. It made me crave those lips. I wanted them to touch me places I wouldn't dare show in public, but I'd venture into voyeurism for him. I sigh and stare down at my cup. I hate Peter and secretly wish I could stab him in his sleep, but I can't deny I'm jealous.

Peter is a beautiful man. His good looks are what drew me to him in the first place, but it was those lips that turned my insides to liquid. I stare at them, unable to look away.

"You okay there, beautiful?" Cass whispers in my ear. He wraps his arms around me from behind and pulls me close.

"Just tired." I lean against him. Guilt stabs me in the side again, a reminder that while I enjoy sex with Cass, it's Peter I think about when I come. Most nights I can push past my thoughts and enjoy the feeling of his body in mine, but tonight I need a break. "I think I'm gonna call it a night."

"Do you want me to walk you up to the tree house?" His voice is a gentle caress against my skin. It's touch unable to break through the barrier I've built tonight.

Watching Peter flaunt his affections with someone else hits harder than I ever could have imagined. I'm angry and hot and on the verge of tears all at once over a man who barely gives me the time of day.

"No. I know the way." I kiss Cass's cheek. If I accept his offer as an escort I'll be pity fucking him tonight and he deserves better. "Thanks though."

I give a small wave to the others and hop off the picnic table before Cass can try and change my mind. Peter and Aria don't notice my departure. They're engrossed in conversation, shamelessly touching each other out in the open. I want to yank her out of his arms by the hair, and that's not me.

All the more reason to leave.

I follow the worn path from the beach to the treehouses. The first time Cass and I walked through the woods, I didn't notice the pressed down grass and dirt covered path we took. Back then, it felt like the forest was closing in on me. The trees dropped their branches low to grab me, they lifted their roots to trip me and the bugs tried to turn me back by attacking.

I was an outsider wandering into uncharted lands. Now, I know when to duck and weave. I know which roots seem to rise and how to avoid walking into a floating swarm of no see ums. I've grown accustomed to the ways of the island. It's accepted me as one of its own and up until this gnawing feeling, I was happy to be one of The Lost it protects.

Cass said everyone here is stuck, forever trapped in their last emotion. If that's true, I don't want to feel like this for all eternity. Full of anger and jealousy. I refuse.

It's time I made a plan to get out of here. No more lingering about. There's nothing useful in Peter's treehouse, and Cass hasn't been forthcoming with more information. But how the hell do I get off of a freaking island?

I stop in my tracks. The answer comes to me and I feel stupid for not having thought of it sooner. I need a boat. Not a boat, those will capsize and sink the moment it comes across a big wave.

What I need is a ship, and I know just where to find one.

CHAPTER 22
Wednesday

"Stars above, Peter, you scared the shit out of me," I say when I recognize the shadow lingering on a tree. I look around, half expecting him to jump out and scare me. Seems like the sort of thing the twisted blend of storybook Peter and broody Mcglare would do.

I don't see him. I cross my arms, irritated by being caught snooping around the far end of the forest. No one told me I couldn't be here, but Cass has avoided this side of the island ever since our jaunt to the pirate cove and everyone else is either with him or on the beach. I'm thinking there's an unwritten rule of where I can and cannot be, which makes the anticipation of what will happen next even worse.

"You can come out now," I tell him, putting my hands on my hips.

The thought that Peter left Aria's side to search for me feeds the jealous bitch in my veins. I fight a smug smile amused that he would leave the comfort of her lips to come find me, especially since I left Cass behind.

Was he hoping to have another run in?

Need pools in my stomach. Peter's knife to my neck turned me on to the point I came within minutes of touching myself. I wonder if he listens outside my door when I whisper his name, wishing it was his fingers beneath my panties instead of mine.

I can't deny there's something between us, an invisible string connecting my lady bits to him. All of him. His glare. His touch. The sound of his breath against my ear.

If he wants a repeat of what happened in the treehouse, or even to take it a step further, I'm game.

"Peter," I call again.

The shadow shakes his head.

I look more closely at the dense foliage around us and realize it's not possible for Peter's shadow to be cast the way it is without standing directly across from it. "Peter isn't here. Is he?"

It shakes his head and then I realize there was some truth to the story. Peter's shadow left him. Maybe that's why he brought me here. Maybe he asked if I was Wendy because he thought that I could reattach it for him.

Stupid man. I could've saved us both a lot of heartache if he would've spoken up instead of assuming, because I'm not Wendy Darling. I don't know how to sew a shadow to a foot.

"Well, I guess this puts us in a predicament doesn't it?" I ask the shadow.

He cocks his head to the side and stares at me. I almost laugh at myself for expecting a verbal answer. Still, I talk to him because if the shadow can follow me and hear me, I need to know if he's on my side or Peter's snitch.

"I want to keep exploring the woods but it seems I've been caught. Are you going to tattle on me?"

Shadow crosses, his arms mimicking my stance, and shakes his head.

"Good. Maybe you and I can be friends, unlike your other half."

Friends with Peter isn't an option for so many reasons I can't count them. For one, he literally kidnapped me. That's a deal breaker in itself, but he's too sexy for his own good and he knows it. The arrogant jerk knew what he was doing, flirting with Aria.

Shadow's shoulders rise and fall, as if he's laughing.

I smirk, unamused that he thinks whatever Peter and I've got going on is comical. I'm about to keep walking when it occurs to me that I'm lost. All of the trees look the same, to the point I'm not sure I could even find my way back to the treehouses.

"Hey, Shadow, do you think you can help me? I'm trying to get to the pirate side of the island."

He shakes his head and viciously waves his arms in an ex-shape, signaling I probably shouldn't go there.

I give him a look, unsure if the shadow can see the *come-on* expression I'm trying to convey or if he just sees my head tilted sideways. "I'm going with or without you. If you're with me, you can make sure I don't get lost along the way. I mean this is Neverland. Isn't it? I'm sure there are carnivorous plants and dangerous animals somewhere on the island. What if I stumble into them because I'm all alone?"

I wait a solid three seconds before marching through the trees again, stepping on broken twigs, listening to them echo in the eternal twilight.

Shadow jumps a couple trunks ahead of me and waves his arms. I fight my smirk, stopping to look at him. He bends over, rests a hand on his knees and wipes sweat from his brows. We have a stare off, if that's what staring at something without eyes can be called, and I think I win.

Shadow sands upright and waves for me to follow him in a different direction. One I'm fairly certain doesn't lead me back to the treehouse or the beach.

"See," I tell him, the pride of knowing he wouldn't let me walk into danger evident in my tone. "I knew you and I would be friends."

If Peter were here, he'd probably be rolling his eyes at me, but considering the shadow has none we walk side-by-side. Him jumping from one tree to the next and me trying not to trip over fallen branches, upturned roots, or my own feet.

We walk and walk, crossing what feels like half the island together. Shadow doesn't attempt to communicate with me and the closer we get to the cove, the more nervous I get.

Cass and I avoided the pirates last time we came. Sure, I saw them, but we didn't talk to anyone. The shops we went to were dead inside and as soon as the one with the large hat got close we left. I don't know what to expect from these people. I'm hoping they're civilized and not misogynistic jerks with bad hygiene.

I decide talking to the shadow, even if he doesn't answer, is better than running scenarios in my mind. If he understands what I'm looking for, maybe he can help me find a way home that doesn't require bartering with the pirates.

"Can I ask you a question, Shadow?" He doesn't motion that he hears me, but I keep talking. "Does Peter think I can attach you to him again?"

Shadow laughs, covering his hand with his belly, dropping his head back. He stops walking for a moment and holds up one finger. I watch him catch his breath and wipe tears I can't see from eyes I'm not sure exist. After a breath or two, the shadow shakes his head.

"Damn. There goes that theory," I say aloud. "Do you know why I'm here?"

Shadow shakes his head again.

"I want to go home," I tell him, letting the longing I've buried deep inside slip into my voice. I held it in so tight, tried to be strong every day that I've been here, make it seem like I don't care even though I'm impatiently trying to count the days until I can see my family again.

I can almost feel the sadness flow from the shadow, which is ridiculous because shadows can't feel. He reaches out in the trees, as if he can touch me, and I extend my hand. Logically I know it's impossible, but right now I feel more alone than I have in my life. I think it's hitting me that if this doesn't work, if I can't find a ship to sail me back to America, I'm going to be on this island for the rest of my life. A life that might be longer and filled with more pain than any existence I could have lived back home.

My fingers touch the darkness that is the shadow's hand, but all I feel is air. His fingers cross into the light. Their dark form turns to dust, disappearing before my eyes. Shadow retracts his hand to the quasi-darkness and holds it up, showing me that he's fine.

I force a smile and nod, relieved that he didn't hurt himself to comfort me, but feel hollow. I start walking again, not in the mood to talk anymore. Shadow leads the way, staying as close to my side as possible without crossing over my own shadow.

The trees around us thin, the forest fading behind us. We step out of the thick and cross a grassy knoll that seems to stretch for an eternity, but I vaguely remember walking it with Cass.

Far ahead, we reach a mountain's edge. Shadow climbs the rock wall. I follow him up, careful to place my hands and feet in the places he does. The ledge we're looking for isn't far, maybe ten feet above us. My arms are screaming when I finally pull myself over the edge. I lay there, my chest tight and out of breath.

I don't remember the climb being this difficult. Or the walk being so far. I furrow my brows, trying to recall details from the first day I was here and frown when I realize a lot of them are gone. "Neverland makes you forget," I whisper to myself, unable to place where I'd heard it before. A movie, maybe? Or perhaps a book. I shudder at the truth of the words and make a mental note to start writing things down. What if I already found the key to getting home, and I forgot it? What else am I forgetting?

I push myself off the cold stone and smile, relieved, when I recognize the red handprint beside a slim opening in the stone. I poke my head into the crack. It's darker than I recall, but I remember the steps. I counted one hundred and twenty-eight from one end to the other. I touch the wall and dew coats my hand. The opening is slim, barely big enough for one person to cross through, sideways, but I had no problem fitting.

I turn sideways, careful not to let my back touch the jagged wall and search for Peter's shadow. He sits at the ledge of the cave, cross legged.

"Are you coming?"

Shadow shakes his head and I can't help but wonder aloud *why*.

Shadow raises hand, like a child making shadow puppets would, and his fingers shift into the shape of a ship.

"You're afraid of boats?"

He shakes his head again. This time he holds his hands above his head to look like a man with a large hat that has a feather on it.

"You don't like pirates."

Shadow nods. Leaving him makes me a little uneasy, but that's why I'm here, to find a captain. "I'll be back soon. Wait for me?"

Shadow shifts back to his Peter-like self and gives me a thumbs up.

This is it. I take a deep breath hoping my nerves will settle. *One way or another, I'm going home.*

CHAPTER 23
Peter

I watch Wednesday leave Cass's side and venture into the woods. It's a struggle not to follow her, not to push her against a tree and claim those lips. Not to touch her sun kissed skin that will forever be a toasted shade of golden brown. Not to trace my fingers down the seam of her tan lines and watch her pretty face twist in pleasure.

Every day I wake, there's a new ripple in my shadow.

A crack in my soul.

I thought I could sit back and let her love another. I thought the years of torture while I stood in the shadows to let my brother woo the girl I loved, only to loose her on this stupid island, had hardened me.

I was wrong.

My shadow's jealousy burns through me, more potent than my own, his rage a second inferno almost as strong. Our feelings are one when it comes to Wednesday and they're making it hard to stay focused.

The only way to break the island's curse is for her to fall in love. I am not an option. My soul is not my own anymore. Cass was supposed to be her new mate, but it's killing me to wait on the sidelines again. I want her. Even if it means condemning The Lost to eternal purgatory, I have to have her.

I sat back and did nothing the first time fate stole my heart.

I won't let it happen again.

CHAPTER 24
Wednesday

W alking through the cove by myself is a different experience than it was when I came with Cass. With him by my side, there was no sense of danger because we passed through the streets like ghosts. This time, it seems like everyone notices me.

I try not to let the wandering eyes shake me. I'm sure the pirates are sharks and can smell fear. I hold my head high, exuding false confidence and read each shop sign. I've passed three saloons, two oddity stores that look to be bursting at the seams with clothes, and a handful of hobby carts.

I decide to take a chance on a saloon called Harper's Edge because I'm sweating. The sky may be the same shade of pinkish blue as it is by the beach, but the sun burns hotter over here. There is no ocean breeze to cool the air even though the cove has a wide mouth and the buildings sit lower than the tree tops.

I thought I had attracted attention on the boardwalk but as I push the swinging doors open it feels like everyone's eyes are on me, my jean shorts, and my Machine Gun Kelly tee shirt. I'm a fish out of water in my converse as everyone in the bar wears boots and jeans or pants that are khaki. The only other girl in the room is behind the bar and even she seems better dressed and I am.

I try not to laugh, fear getting the best of me, because it looks like I traveled back in time five hundred years to the era of Blackbeard and all his Scally wags.

"What can I get yeh," the bartender asks, her accent heavy but indiscernible.

"What do you have?" The only thing I've drank on this island is water and faery wine and I have a feeling that neither of them are served at this bar.

"Yer new around here, ain't yeh?"

"Is it that obvious?"

"Yeh, love." She laughs and pulls two wooden mugs from beneath the counter. "Yeh got a tongue for the stout stuff or are yer a weaklin'?"

I'm not a fan of shots, and drinks like jack and coke make me cringe. I want to enjoy my alcohol, not swallow fire. I also know that this is a test and even if I have to hold my breath to down whatever she gives me, I'll do it. "Surprise me."

The girl chuckles and pulls the cork out of a small barrel, letting its dark liquor pour into the cup. I have a feeling it's gonna taste like fire, but thank her anyway.

"That'll be ten shillings," she says, sliding the cup across a teak countertop.

I stare at her, eyes wide. Money was never an option on the beach. We've ate and drank and lived on the left side of civilization and so I have nothing to offer. "Oh, I'm sorry, I don't ..."

Someone sets a silver coin on the counter beside me. "I've got her, Melinda."

"Thank you," I say looking up at pale blue eyes encircled by a thick layer of charcoal. The man's lips lift, revealing two dimples, with a thick scar going through one. I blush, as I take in the dark stubble on his jaw and the gold hoop in his ear.

"Haven't seen yeh around these parts," he says in an accent that's either English or Scottish or something ending in -ish. My knowledge of dialects goes as far as movies and audiobooks and for all I know they are wrong, but this man's voice is *right*.

I'm embarrassed to find him attractive and doubt someone with so much swagger would look twice at me. But those sky blue eyes trail over my body, stopping on my chest before reaching my face again.

I shiver, goosebumps peppering my skin, and not in a bad way. It reminds me of the way Peter made me feel in Florida, full of excitement and desire with an added familiarity that we've met before, but I would recognize him if we'd crossed paths in the past and I'm sure we haven't.

"Seems like I might need to dress better in these parts of the woods." I smile down at the drink I'm too scared to try. What is it with this island and men? Every one of them, down to the hobo looking one in the corner, is breathtaking. Possibly in need of a shower, but still beautiful. I lean closer to the one beside me, playfully whispering, "Everyone keeps looking at me."

"I assure yeh, Sunshine, it's not because of yer clothes." He holds a finger up and the bartender hands him a mug filled with something yellow and frothy.

"Sunshine?" I ask, enamored with the pet name.

"Aye. Yer beautiful, casting a ray of golden light, but dangerous to anyone who looks too long." He winks and chugs half his drink.

I hide the heat of my cheeks by lifting my own cup. The smell of my drink singes my nostrils. Whatever came out of the barrel is going to be hell to swallow. I take a small sip. The alcohol attacks my throat with flames from hell. It's more bitter than black coffee and takes every bit of will power I have not to spit it out.

He laughs, bellowing out a deep chuckle. "That's precious, Sunshine. Never seen anyone make a face like that while drinking."

"Fuck you." I reach for his drink, convinced it will be better than my own. He lets me steal the rest and I'm relieved when it tastes like butterscotch. I gasp for air, fire still burning my lungs.

"Generally speaking, I like to know the names of the lasses I swap spit with." He flashes me a set of pearly whites and holds out his hand. "The name's James Panton."

"Wednesday." I set my hand in his and he shakes it with a firm grip. "Roberts."

"Well, Ms. Roberts, it is a pleasure to meet you. Would yeh like another round?"

"Of what you're drinking? Sure. But this..." I slide my nearly full cup to the side. "No thank you."

James chuckles. He takes my mug and tosses the contents back as if it were an oversized shot. He winces as he swallows, but the moment the cup is on the counter again it's like he just drank water.

Melinda brings us two full glasses of the butterscotch beer, then leaves us to tend to the man who's fallen asleep on her table across the room.

"Dance with me," James says without warning. He stands and holds his hand out for me to take.

"There's no music." Even as I protest I find myself agreeing to the request. The least I can offer is an awkward dance after he bought me two and a half drinks.

"So long as our heart beats there is music in our souls." He spins me once then pulls me close to his chest. We sway, slow stepping to a melody he hums.

"Are all the pirates as nice as you?"

He smirks and dips me backward. "There is no other like me." We're upright again, my hand enclosed in his, resting against his chest. I can feel the slow steady beat of his heart. "Why? Looking fer new company already."

"I'm sorry. I don't mean to be rude."

"Apology accepted."

James twirls me around the bar floor. We skirt around empty tables and chairs. The eyes that look at us when we draw near avert their gaze, as if they're afraid. I notice but keep the observation to myself, curiosity getting the best of me.

"It's just... I'm in search of a captain."

"Yer in luck. I have a ship." He kisses my hand and we stop dancing.

My heart is racing both from the excitement of maybe finding someone to take me home and being in his arms. We take our seats again and I'm surprised to find our drinks are still cold.

"Where is it yer wanting to go?"

"To Florida."

My answer makes him pause mid sip. James sets his drink on the bar top and stares at me, his eyes taking me in with more than surface interest. "A journey like that is no easy task."

"I know, and I don't have much to offer."

"I'll make it easy on yeh. Go on a date with me, Sunshine, and I'll take yeh to the moon if that's what yeh want." He takes no time in thinking about a reply.

I chew on my bottom lip. I'm already in over my head juggling Cass and these unresolved feelings for Peter. I know myself. Give me a few drinks and an evening filled with good conversation and dancing and my lady bits will be begging for a ride.

But I'm turning into the person I swore I wouldn't be.

James sees the hesitation on my face and grins. He takes my hand and presses his lips to my knuckles as he stands. "There's no pressure, but if yeh decide to take me up on my offer all yeh need to do is return to Harper's Edge and I will find you."

"You make this sound easy."

"And yer making a single night with me more than it is. I promise I don't bite, unless yer into that sort of thing."

James winks and I shove his chest. The look he gives me in that moment strikes a chord deep inside. I've seen it before, somewhere, only I can't place when or how.

"Until we meet again."

CHAPTER 25
Wednesday

Navigating back to the treehouse is harder than I anticipated, even with the shadow's help. My brain is fuzzy from the butterscotch beer, but I feel good. My skin is warm and my body buzzes with life.

I hum a melody similar to the one James and I danced to. I think tonight is the most fun I've had since coming to Neverland. Even as I tried to negotiate a way home, the constant blanket of stress I carry when it comes to Peter and Cass was set aside. It was nice.

But as I stare up at the ladder that leads to the spider web of rope bridges, I feel that blanket falling on my shoulders again. The only relief I have is the small sliver of hope that James will honor his word. One date that may or may not lead to more, and I'll be on a ship sailing far, far away.

I climb the steps of the ladder and then crawl across the bridge to Peter's door. This is another thing I can't imagine doing for the rest of my life, crawling like a helpless imp. I stand, my breaths ragged, and open the door.

I couldn't see the lights on from outside.

I didn't know that the treehouse wasn't empty.

I stand in the open door, my jaw dropped, unable to tear my gaze away from Peter's naked body. The hard lines of his muscles, shadowed by ink or hair are beautiful. I swallow hard as my eyes dip lower. There's a bar with a small silver ball on each end going through the head of his dick. I've never felt anything like that inside me before. I stare at him and all his glory, wondering if he's always that big, or if he's a grower and there's more to come.

"I'm sorry," I whisper. My cheeks burn red. I step inside, quickly closing the door, and cover my face with my hands.

Peter chuckles and the deep rumble of his voice makes me ache to be touched. I hate how much I still want him. All those anti-hero books I read have ruined me.

"Is Aria around?" I manage to ask. I force myself to find a mental picture of them together on the beach. If I focus on the feeling I felt, I might be able to make it to my room without soaking my panties.

"Why would she be?"

"I don't know, I just assumed you and her..." I peek through my fingers hoping Peter's disappeared to put clothes on. He's standing in front of me, inches away. I flinch, involuntarily, and his *thing* touches my leg. The soft head brushes a thin layer of stickiness on my skin, and I can't help but wonder if he's hard for me.

"Assuming things can get you in a lot of trouble." Peter grabs my wrists and tugs my arms down. He holds them at my sides. I take a step back, bumping into the door, but he's still barely a breath away.

"I... I should go to my room."

"Probably." He smirks and I get the feeling I'm in for a ride. "Answer me one question and you're free to go."

Would he keep me here if I don't? Better question, do I want him to? "What?"

He leans close, his breath tickling my ear and whispers, "Is it my name on the tip of your tongue when Cass is tunneling into you?"

I swallow hard, not wanting to admit that his name *is* the one I want to cry out. I enjoy Cass, he makes me feel good, but he doesn't give me *this* feeling, the one where I'm standing on the edge of a cliff about to fall into something I know I'm not ready for.

Peter's hand closes around my throat, his touch gentle yet firm. "Truth or dare?"

I don't respond.

"I dare you to kiss me," he says, with the quick lift of his lips.

I can't even blink before his mouth is on mine. I don't fight against his tongue sweeping past my lips. I fist his hair and pull him closer. Our teeth clank. This isn't a sweet kiss full of hope and desires. It's pure lust. A primal need to be satisfied his lips are only grazing. I drop my hand between us and wrap my fingers around this shaft. I stroke his thickness, moaning against his lips because touching him turns me on.

Peter bites my lip. I gasp, the pain sharp but enjoyable. "Truth or dare," he asks again.

"Truth."

He takes a micro-step back and I let him go. "Did you enjoy that?"

"Did you?" Without breaking eye contact, I wipe the beads of pre-come that coat my palm against my shorts.

Peter glances down at the hard thickness poking against my thigh. There's a question hanging in the air I want him to ask. I wait longer than I should before saying, "I'm going to bed."

Peter steps to the side. I won't deny I'm disappointed. Peter is the kind of man mothers warn their daughters to stay away from. The kind that have to be experienced before they can be washed out of their system. I need to cleanse myself of this addiction, strange and unwanted as it may be, and the only way to do that is by giving into it first.

"Darling?" he purrs just before I reach my room.

I grip the doorframe. He once said he could read my expression, well I want to keep these feelings to myself. If we're going to fuck, it's going to be on my terms, not when he's dangling what I want most on a string, just out of reach.

"Do you believe in love?"

"Why?" I look over my shoulder. I expect a cocky grin, but he stares at me with interest, pure curiosity in his eyes and I can't resist asking, "Are you falling in love with me?"

"You'd be so lucky, darling. If I loved you the stars would shine and the sun would rise." He doesn't laugh or give me that condescending breathy chuckle I despise. "You didn't answer my question."

I watch him, waiting for the shoe to drop but he simply waits. He doesn't move across the room, or lift his lips in a smile. He doesn't shift to lean against the door, or ruffle his hair. He just stands there. Waiting. "Yes, Peter, I believe in love."

He finally smiles, but the sight tugs at my heart. I've never seen something so sad. "Good."

CHAPTER 26
Wednesday

Peter's words haunt me.

I don't know why. It was just a question, one that would be normal in any other setting, but it's kept me up all night, tossing and turning, thinking about what it would be like to fall in love again.

Would it make me ache to be touched? Or would that need be satisfied without asking. Would love cause me to be short tempered and want to smack him whenever I'm around? Or would our lips crash together in a heated kiss that makes me weak in the knees every time we felt like fighting?

I roll onto my side and find Peter's shadow sitting on the silhouette of the chair, watching me. His presence is an odd comfort, but the fact that he can't soothe my skin makes me long for touch even more.

"Can he fall in love?" I ask, knowing the question will go unanswered.

"I owe you a truth." Peter's deep rumble carries from the hallway. I push onto my elbows. He stands, arms crossed in the doorway, his shoulder leaning against the frame. "Is that the question you want to ask?"

My chest rises and falls chaotically as he crosses into my room. My heart picks up speed with every thump of the heel of his boot against the wood floor. He grips the footboard of the bed, long, thick fingers curling over the wood.

"Going out?" I ask. I don't think I'll ever get used to the sight of Peter's naked body. Dark denim covers his legs and hugs his ass, but his chest is bare and the effect on me is the same.

"Ask me to stay and I won't." Peter says, his voice carrying a hidden question. I have a feeling this moment will change everything between us. He leans closer, his body inching over mine, waiting for me to make the next move.

I swallow hard, unable to tear my gaze from his. I feel it again, that nervous fire igniting inside me, growing into an all consuming blaze that demands to be touched. "Stay," I whisper.

Peter pounces, moving like a predator in the night. He covers me, his body pressing against mine while his fingers thread through my hair, mouth crashing against mine. His kiss is hungry, demanding, and yet gentle. There's a hesitation in his lips that makes me angry.

I hook my legs around Peter's waist. He snaps. Gentle fingers turn rough. He fists my hair and pulls my lips from his. Teeth sink into my shoulder. The pain is sharp but not unbearable. I close my eyes and arch my back, surprised at how thin the line between pleasure and pain is.

Peter takes the neck of my night shirt and tugs, ripping it down the center until my chest is exposed. "You're perfect."

He kisses the swell of my breast. Sucks my nipple into his mouth. I stare up at the ceiling, struggling to keep my breaths controlled. Peter slides his hand under my pajama shorts and presses a finger into my center. I gasp, on the brink of coming from his touch.

"Not yet, Darling," he whispers, then sucks the lobe of my ear into his mouth. "You're not allowed to come until I'm inside you. Understand?"

I chew on my bottom lip and nod, unsure how I'm going to meet his demands. I'm so close already, forcing myself to hold back is torture. He kisses the sensitive spot of my neck and presses a second finger inside. "Good girl."

I close my eyes and focus on my breathing, forcing myself to keep a slow steady rhythm. Peter kisses down my chest, stopping to suck my nipple between his teeth, then continues to make his way south.

He pulls his fingers from my folds and yanks my shorts off. I barely have time to take a breath before his mouth is between my legs. He sucks on my clit and I scream his name, unable to stop the sensation running through me. I grip his hair and pull his face closer, desperate to feel more.

"I need you," I say through heavy breaths. "Please, Peter, I can't take much more."

He lifts his face and slides up my body. He fists my hair again and pulls my mouth to his, parting my lips with his tongue, sweeping it inside me. "Do you like the way you taste, Darling?"

I hum against his lips.

"Words, sweetheart."

I barely get the yes out before he's slamming his cock inside me. There's no slow, gentle teasing. His hips thrust in and out, shoving his dick painfully deep, and yet I can't help the sound of pleasure leaving my lips. Peter pulls me upwards, and I bounce on his lap. His hand roams my back, side, chest while his tongue tastes my lips.

"Oh, god, Peter, I'm—"

"No," he demands.

Peter grips my hips and throws me off of him, onto the mattress. He flips me onto my stomach and lifts my ass until he's happy with the angle, then sinks into me again. I scream, the pleasure instant. Peter's fingers wrap around my neck as he pounds into me. My walls tighten around his length and I come first, harder than I ever have. The slick, slapping sound of his balls against my clit almost makes me come again but he pulls out once more, and turns me on my back again.

"You're so fucking wet," he says against my lips. He drops a hand between our bodies and rubs my clit as he grows harder inside me.

"Fuck me," I breathe, heat growing inside me. I'm going to come again, for the third time in a row. Pressure builds in my center, the need to release, to push greater than anything I've felt before. I give in to the sensation, euphoria claiming my body as my come gushes out of me, coating Peter's dick, balls, and bed sheets.

"Fuck, baby." His chest rises and falls. He digs his fingers into my skin, pulling me closer to him as he thrusts, deeper, harder, until his seed coats every inch of my insides.

Peter pulls out and rolls beside me. He extends one arm and I lay beside him. We stay there, catching our breaths.

"Do you regret it?" His tone is rough, but I hear the insecurity behind the bravado.

I press my palm to his cheek and turn his face to look at me. "It was perfect." Everything I thought sleeping with Peter would be like and more. I close my eyes and let myself fall into a new feeling. Peacefulness. A strange calm that makes me feel like I've finally found the person I'm meant to be with.

As I doze off, I don't think about the events that brought us here or how I need to get home. I don't worry about the tomorrows, what this means for Peter and I or what I'm going to tell Cass, if anything.

I curl into Peter's side, his arm wrapping to hold me close, and fall into the deepest, most restful sleep I've had since coming to Neverland.

CHAPTER 27
Peter

I wake to a banging on the front door. *Thump. Thump. Thump.* I groan, and wait, hoping whoever is out front will leave, but they're persistent. They keep pounding, and pounding, until finally I decide to get up.

I slide my arm from underneath Wednesday, careful not to wake her. For a second, I stand there and just look at how beautiful she is. The soft rouge of her lips. Her butterfly lashes. The soft curves of her body.

She's perfection.

And she's mine.

The pounding outside continues. I grab a towel from the bathroom and wrap it around my waist. I unlatch the front door lock and yank it open. "What?" I demand.

"What the fuck did you do?" Cass asks, his tone laced with equal venom. His eyes narrow on me and the terrycloth at my waist.

"Nothing yet. I was going to take a shower, but you've fucked that up," I quip. I take a breath, not meaning to be short with Cass. It's not his fault I hate him. I pushed him into a relationship with Wednesday. I presented him with the forbidden fruit, hoping he'd take a bite, then hated when he fell under its spell. If I'm honest, I don't hate Cass. I hate myself for letting Wednesday be with anyone besides me. But he's a better target to lash out at. "What do you mean, *what the fuck did I do?*"

Cass steps to the side and I don't know how I didn't notice the moment the door opened. Darkness falls over Neverland, blanketing our island in dark hues and the glow of the moon. I step onto the porch and look up, eyes wide with wonder as I see the stars in the land I call home for the first time in centuries.

"We need to call a meeting," Cass insists. "The Lost are freaking out. They've never seen the island in anything but twilight."

He's right. But I'm not ready to move. I count the constellations and find true North, then spot the second star to the right and grin. Wendy's favorite star in the sky. I don't know if it has a name. I'm sure it does since humans claim everything they can, but Wendy used to call it the wishing star. It was there she sent her deepest desires and hoped they'd come true. I stare up at it and send a wish of my own. *Forgive me.*

"Peter," Cass huffs.

"Let me get dressed." I grab the edge of the door and meet Cass's gaze. He knows what I've done. I can see it in his eyes but I don't have the courage to voice my actions. Not yet. Soon, everyone will know but for now I want this moment between us to be mine. "I'll be out in a minute."

I shut the door, feeling Cass's frustration come through the wall. I cross into the kitchen and grab a frosted glass and fill it with water. The cold chill does nothing to soothe the fire beneath my skin. It burns, like a parasite stretching my soul to make room for his.

I freeze, realizing the sensation and look behind me.

My shadow is attached, following my every movement. I lift my leg, wave my arm, and he does what I wish without protest. I lean against the counter and stare at it. My thoughts are empty, void of rude interruptions. I kind of miss them, as odd as it seems. My shadow and I may not have agreed on much but he was my ally. The only being I could truly trust.

And now he's gone.

I run my hand over my face and take a deep breath. I'm not used to so many feelings kicking up at once. Longing. Sorrow. Worry. And most heavily, love.

I pad back into Wednesday's room. I wonder if she'll realize what's happened. Her precious mind runs a mile a minute, and I left enough bread crumbs.

I brush my fingers against her cheek, pushing her wild locks aside, then kiss her skin. She stirs with a half conscious moan. "I have to step out for a bit."

"Where are you going?" She rolls onto her back, butterfly lashes fluttering, trying to stay open.

"Island bullshit. Go back to sleep. I'll see you when you wake."

"You sure?"

I kiss her lips. She smiles against my mouth. I feel the lasso around my heart tightening. The longer Wednesday is here the more dangerous it is for her. Now that the Island has shifted, our time together is even shorter than it should be. "Positive. Rest, Darling."

I stand but she reaches for my hand. "Peter?"

"Yes, love?"

"Tell me the truth, there's something here, isn't there?" She hesitates and her big browns reach mine. "I'm not imagining it. Right?"

"What we have is more than *something*, Darling. So much more."

CHAPTER 28
Wednesday

I've woken in this bed every day for what feels like a lifetime, but I've never had a reason to smile like I do today. I roll on my side and hug the sheets. They still smell like him. Any doubts that last night was a dream erased.

I need to tell Cass, I think to myself, the quick upturn of my lips falling. He may be all right with sharing me, but I'm not that girl. I don't think Peter would be down for that either.

I take a quick shower then put on a fresh set of clothes. The treehouse seems darker, but the shadows don't phase me. Clouds crossing over the sky create a similar darkness. I don't think anything of it until I step outside.

The moon, nearly full, smiles down on me. The stars twinkle around the nearly round sphere. It's breathtaking. This must be what Peter meant when he said he had to deal with island problems.

I run down to the beach to find him. The glow of a fire greets me through the trees, the sound of eighties music bouncing off the leaves. I step out of the brush, surprised to find The Lost drinking and celebrating.

"Wednesday!" Scarlett says loud enough for me to hear her over the music. I'm shocked. This girl barely whispers and now she's yelling my name with excitement, "You're here."

She hands Heidi her drink and runs over to me, pulling me into a hug. I'm so taken back I don't know what to do. "Hey, Scar," I manage to say,

"Do you see the moon?" She drops her head back and looks up at the sky. "It's the most glorious thing. Don't you think so?"

"It's something." Probably bad based on what Cass told me about the island. "Have you seen Peter?"

"Don't you mean Cass?" she asks, a twinkle in her eye.

"I don't know if I'm ready—"

"Ready to what, beautiful?" Cass asks, his arms snaking around my waist from behind.

"Oh, hey." I turn to look at him and he kisses me. My stomach drops. I feel guilty, like I'm doing something wrong even though Peter and I haven't had the conversation about what we are. And we *are* something. I can feel it like I feel the air in my lungs. The question is... what?

I break the kiss before Cass's tongue can try to part my lips and spin in his arms. "I was just saying I don't know if I'm ready for a drink yet. I haven't eaten anything since I got up."

I lick my lips and don't like the sour flavor his left behind.

"We can fix that." Cass takes my hand and guides me to the fire.

I feel eyes on me, but every time I look up no one seems to be looking at us. The Lost are happily dancing or talking with each other.

I take the plate of grilled corn and the roll Cass hands me and force a smile. I'm being paranoid. No one knows Peter and I slept together, and if they figure it out then so what. From what Xyris said, The Lost swap partners anyway. Why can't I?

A pit swells in my stomach and suddenly I'm not so hungry. Images of Peter fucking the other girls assault my mind. Him railing Aria from behind. Heidi riding his dick while he eats out Scarlett. I force myself to take a bite of bread and struggle to keep it down.

"Are you okay?" Cass takes the plate and touches my forehead with the back of his head. "You don't look so good."

"I'm fine," I insist. I'm not sure he believes me. A thin layer of sweat coats my skin. I can't make the pictures go away. Can't stop seeing Scarlett's *O* face in my mind. "A little thirsty."

"Hang tight." Cass steps to the picnic table and fills a cup with something deep red. "Best faery wine of the season."

I swallow half the glass in one gulp, half listening to him ramble about cherries and pomegranates. The first wave of euphoria hits within minutes and silences my thoughts. I finish the glass, finally able to breathe easy and ask for another.

Cass laughs, his voice an incomprehensible sound of deep rumble and blurred music. He takes my hand and leads us both to a picnic table. He lifts me onto the table and fills my cup again.

I'm lost in the feeling of electricity buzzing beneath my skin. I can feel the blood rushing in my veins. It tingles, like when my foot falls asleep and I wake it without warning, but instead of the sensation being painful it carries heat to the best parts of my body and turns me on.

Cass says something about regret and I snap my gaze to his.

"Wednesday!" Xyris calls. He and Emmit cross the sand, their lips swollen, hair a tousled mess. "I've got to know something."

"What's that, handsome?" I surprise myself with the compliment but let it go because it is the truth. Xyrs is gorgeous. Everyone I've met on the island is.

"Are you named after the murderous little girl from the nineties?" he asks.

"No." I laugh. "That would have been cool. I was named after hump day because my mom knew I'd grow up to hump a bunch of things."

Emmit bursts out laughing, his head drops back as he howls.

"What's so funny?" Aria asks, walking up with the girls.

"Inside joke. Had to be there." Xyris shrugs in reply.

Heidi flips him the bird, a large grin on her face. I don't think I've ever seen her smile. She's pretty when she's not being a bitch.

"Stars and scars, Cass." Aria giggles. "What did you give her?" She takes my cup and tosses the red stuff on the ground. "No more of that or you'll likely tell us all your dirty secrets."

My eyes go wide, realizing I said that out loud. I look to Heidi, an apology on her lips. She smirks against her glass and rolls her eyes. "No hard feelings, Darling."

"Here." Aria hands me a drink that looks like the stars, clear with glistening bits throughout. "This one is my favorite. It's made with dragonfruit."

"Easy now," Heidi warns. "That shit's like a pissed off ex-girlfriend, sweet as can be until it's time for something new. Take it slow."

"Oh, look." Aria covers her heart with both hands. "She cares."

Heidi flips Aria a vulgar gesture. She grins then looks at me side eyed. "What can I say, the little bitch has grown on me."

I've drank half the glass already. It went down smooth, which is probably why I'm smiling, enjoying the songs on the radio, not caring to explore or probe for information.

"I've got to know," I finally ask. "Why are you using that dinosaur and not a bluetooth speaker?"

"No wifi," Aria says. She tips some of her wine into my almost empty cup. "The island is a dead zone. But we have an insane amount of cassette tapes and rechargeable batteries connected to a solar charger."

"The downside of island living," Heidi adds.

"It's not so bad. You get used to the slower way of life," Scarlett chimes in.

"I wish things could stay like this forever," Cass whispers into my ear, his voice full of longing and sadness.

I forgot he was beside me. The wine is good. Too good. My head feels heavy and it's hard to keep my eyes open. I don't know why. I was fine a moment ago but something feels different. Wrong.

"Cass." I look for him, but he's no longer at my side. I don't know when he left. He was here a second ago. I think. My vision blurs. The world becoming a swirl of lights and colors.

Someone touches my cheek and I hear my name, but the voice sounds far away and worried.

Strong hands grip my arms. I force my eyelids to lift, expecting to see Cass steadying me, but dark eyes meet mine. I shiver as Peter's gaze burns a hole in me. I remember why I like him so much. He's stunningly handsome, even more so than the others.

I reach up and touch his cheek. My hand hits his skin harder than I anticipate. It smacks against his jaw. I wonder if he likes it rough. If next time I should slap him and see if it makes him tunnel deeper into me.

"How much have you drank tonight?" I hear the worry in his voice but can't do anything but grin.

"Two dragon fruits and a red wine Cass gave her," Scarlet replies. There's a change in the air. A tension I can't place.

"We should go." Peter takes my hands in his. My legs give out as I slide off the table. He catches me before I fall and lifts me effortlessly.

"I don't understand," Aria mumbles. "I cut the wine to an eighth of its potency. It shouldn't have done this to her."

Peter grunts in response.

"I'm sorry," she pleads. He ignores her, carrying me past our friends. "Peter, I'm sorry!"

No one tries to stop him as he carries me into darkness. I roll into his chest and reach up to touch his cheek. "Don't be mad at her, baby. I'm just a little drunk. I'm all right."

Peter ignores me. The crunch of his boots over fallen twigs the only sound between us.

"Baby?" I ask, a crushing sadness filling me.

"Shhh," he whispers. "You'll be okay. As soon as we get some water in you, you'll be all right." But there's something about the way he says it that makes me nervous.

Peter climbs the ladder to his tree house that's set in the middle of their camp while the others span out like webs from a spider's web. He walks us through the front door and up the stairs, back to my room, and lays me in the bed.

He disappears into the bathroom and returns with a damp rag and a cup of water. He sets the rag on the back of my neck and insists I drink.

I sit upright and take the glass. As soon as I take the first sip my stomach doesn't feel right. Something inside me flips, the feel good sensation turns into a world spinning, thunder roaring ache. I hold my belly, hoping that the turmoil inside settles. "Oh, god."

There's no time. Liquid pain climbs my throat, dragging a whirl-wind of emotions and the wine I drank along for the ride. I race for the bathroom but my legs give out. I puke all over myself and the floor.

CHAPTER 29
Wednesday

"Y*ou're too good to keep.*"

My head spins. Skin hurts. I open my eyes and there's Peter again, sitting backwards on the chair, watching me sleep. The room is dark, lit only by a lantern on the bedside table.

"Your such a fucking creeper." I groan as I try to sit up. My muscles are too weak. Too tired.

"Eat." He slides a plate of toast over.

I try to laugh but it comes out closer to a whimper.

"What happened? I feel like I walked off a cliff."

"If you do, make sure I'm there."

"Why? So you can catch me." I wink but he doesn't take the bait. Peter stares at me, a deep set frown on his lips. I push onto my elbows and touch his hands. "What's wrong?"

"What do you remember about the other night?"

"Not much. Why?"

"You've been out cold for two days. I was worried the wine got the best of you. I thought..." He shakes his head.

"Two days!" I sit all the way up and instantly regret it. I lay back down and groan. "What the hell was in that...Oh, god." I cover my hand with my mouth and look for something, anything to throw up in.

Peter is ready and waiting with a bucket. I hate that I need him, but I'm grateful for his presence. He fists my hair, holding it out of the way while I hurl. There's nothing left in my stomach. Yellow bile burns my throat. When it runs out, I dry heave a few more times before my body gets the memo to quit. I fall back onto the pillow, more tired than I was when I woke up.

Peter sets a cold cloth on the back of my neck. He holds a cup with a straw in front of me. "Rinse your mouth out."

I swish the cold water around and spit into the bucket, then do it again before swallowing a small amount.

"You need to eat, Wednesday. You're too weak." Peter picks pieces of the toast apart and holds it in front of me. "Please."

I hate that he's right, but I eat it anyway. "If you wanted to get me in bed again all you had to do is ask," I tease, trying to lighten the mood.

Peter smiles and wipes my hair from my face. "Another time, Darling." He pinches off another bite and feeds it to me.

"Promise?" I groan, my stomach cramping again and roll on my side to face him. I look at the darkness floating in the blue of his irises, then close my eyes.

"I'll fuck you until the bed breaks if that's what you want." He strokes my head, pushing my hair away from my face. I feel so drained. It's getting harder to stay awake. "But you've got to stay awake, Darling, don't give in."

"Do you believe in soulmates, Peter?" My eyes drift closed, the dark void of sleep calling to me. "Because I feel complete when I'm with you."

"Darling, don't do that." Peter taps my cheek. He sounds so far away, his touch so light I can barely feel it. "Wake up, Wednesday. Come on. Stay with me." His voice breaks, and it's the last sound I hear before letting myself drift back into nothingness.

CHAPTER 30
Wednesday

Thunder cracks in the sky.

Flashes of yellow light flickers through the room, cutting through the darkness. I don't know how long I've been awake, laying here, waiting for my voice, my legs, any part of me to listen to my brain. It's a terrifying feeling, being trapped in your own body, your mind awake and full of life while the rest of you is listless.

Little by little, the spell on my limbs lifts. My toes wiggle, my fingers open and close. Rain cascades down the window, each rumble in the night bringing life to my body again.

I'm not sure how long it takes, time seems to move on its own, crawling by, but eventually I'm able to sit up. My arms feel like lead, heavy and awkward to move. My legs as impossible to wield as Thor's hammer.

Step by tremulous step I cross the room. Fire burns in my lungs. Something so simple as walking twenty feet shouldn't be so exhausting, but I'm drained. I collapse against the doorframe, half ready to give up and fall to the floor.

Peter's eyes lock on mine the moment I break through the shadows veiling my room, his face a mix of shock and terror. He shuts his book and jumps out of the chair to be by my side. "What... what are you doing?"

Peter ducks under my arm and holds me by my waist. His scent—the same rich mix of earth and sage—fills my veins. It takes me back to a day that feels like a lifetime ago when he filled me as thoroughly as his cologne does.

Peter practically carries me to a nearby chair, my legs barely working, and helps me find a comfortable position. He kneels in front of me, his deep blues searching my face. The longer he stares, the more I don't like what I see in return. His lips press together into a tight frown and his eyebrows pull together. "You shouldn't be walking around. You'll drain yourself."

"I didn't want to lay there anymore." My voice cracks from lack of use. I sound like a woman who smokes a pack a day, raspy. Nothing like myself.

"How long have you been awake?"

That's the question of the day. How long did I lay there motionless, unable to control my body or scream out for help? My room was dark when I finally found the strength to open my eyes, leaving one vast stretch of nothingness for another. I didn't dream while I rested, or if I did I can't remember. "A while."

Peter's frown deepens. "I wanted to be there when you came around again. I'm sorry I wasn't."

"Was I asleep long?" I feel like I know the answer. I wouldn't be this sore if I had simply slept for an evening. Something happened to me. I need Peter to tell me what.

"You should eat something," he deflects. "Build your strength up again."

My stomach cramps at the mention of food. The pain spreads from below my belly button around to my back, violently alerting me that it's hungry.

I nod tired again and close my eyes as Peter walks to the kitchenette behind me. Cabinets open and close as he gathers his items. I focus on my breathing. My chest is heavy, but I force my lungs to take in air and then let it out. Existing shouldn't be this painful.

Peter brushes his fingers down the side of my arm, his touch gentle, as if he were caressing the petals of a rose.

I open my eyes and smile. Peter looks down at me with worried eyes, but returns the gesture. He lowers to his knees, a small brown cup in his hands, and sits on his heels. "Careful, the tea is hot."

He hands me the cup and places his hands over mine, helping me lift it to my lips, tilting it slowly. The liquid is pleasantly warm, sweetened with honey, and smells of lavender. It soothes the cracks in my throat, making swallowing an easy task instead of a chore.

"Thank you," I rasp, feeling a little more like myself after a few sips.

"Hang on." Peter brings both our hands to my lap until the cup rests on my legs. He gets up and practically runs to the kitchen to grab a small, cardboard box. "Cass brought these by this morning."

Peter lifts two blueberry muffins out and sets them on a wooden plate. He finds his place in front of me again and takes my cup, setting the muffins in its place on my lap.

"He'll probably be back once the rain stops to check on you again." Peter's lips lift into a sad smile. "I...uh... didn't feel right telling him about us while you were out. He still thinks he has a chance with you." Peter hesitates and I can see the worry in his eyes again. "Does he, Darling?"

"I don't feel right," I confess. I'm not trying to avoid the question but something inside me isn't as it was before. It's hard to pinpoint what is different. My arms and legs aren't as heavy, but it's not a physical change that's weighing on me. It's something else. A heaviness on my heart, a pinpoint hole in my soul.

"You gave Death a run for his money. I'd be surprised if he let you get away unscathed." Peter doesn't look at me as he tears the muffin into pieces and feeds it to me. I think he's trying to be playful and show me the side of him I glimpsed so long ago, but there's a dark cloud hovering over us. His glee feels forced.

"You scared me, Wednesday." Peter swallows hard. Bloodshot eyes meet mine. They're glossy, filled with tears he refuses to release. He closes his eyes again. Lets out a shaky breath. "You were in and out of consciousness for a week. I thought we were going to lose you."

"I don't understand." I press the palm of my hand to my forehead. A dull ache pools behind my eyes. How could a week have passed? It doesn't seem possible. "The last thing I remember is sitting by the bonfire."

I cup Peter's cheeks and lift his face until he has to look at me. The man, who's only ever shown me confidence, is lost. He's a shell of the person I've grown to hate. A broken boy on his knees. "I'm okay," I whisper.

He shakes his head. "I don't know that you are, Wednesday."

Hearing my name on his lips is jarring. Peter has only ever called me Darling. But it's his words that make me shiver. I can say the words all day long but he's right. There's something missing. I can't explain what or how I know, but there's a void where that piece once was.

I lean down and kiss Peter's lips. He doesn't let me linger. His arms wrap around my waist. He holds me the way I'd expect him to if this were goodbye. Tears pool in my eyes and slowly run down my cheeks as I realize he thought we wouldn't see each other again. The severity of how close I was to dying again shakes me to the core.

This whole time I wanted nothing more than to leave Neverland but now, I can't imagine saying goodbye.

CHAPTER 31
Wednesday

Days pass, the sun rising and falling more times than I care to count, but with each change of the sky I grow stronger. Able to walk further and stay awake longer. Dying twice—or coming close to it—took more out of me than I could have imagined but I'm still here.

Neverland is gonna have to try harder if it wants me as one of The Lost.

I haven't seen Cass yet. I've been awake for days yet he and the others keep missing me, or so Peter says. He claims they've stopped by when I've been sleeping but I don't buy it. I've been awake for what I think is a week and haven't napped once. I think they're hiding something.

Especially Cass.

I doubt Peter would tell him we slept together while I've been recovering. His default mode may be dick-head, but he's not heartless. Cass is his friend. Besides, he would have told me if that conversation happened. Something else is going on and I want to know what.

I sit beside the window, one of Peter's books in my hand, waiting for him to return. His library is more versed than I originally thought. While it's mostly classics there's a few shelves that make me grin, specifically the cheesy romance novels with Fabio-men on the covers.

I'm on my second novel and the stories themselves haven't been bad so far. If I ever make it home, I'm going to raid my mother's books. She's been dying for me to read some author with the last name Ward, but I couldn't get past the covers. I smirk and turn the page of my book. I bet she's a smut reader from way back.

My ears recognize the creak of the hinges on the front door. I dog-ear my page and close the book. The sun casts shadows that are directly below the leaves. If I was to guess, I'd say it's almost noon. It's still weird to see it rise and fall in Neverland. We haven't talked about what caused the change. Peter's danced around a lot of my questions the past few days.

"Hello, Darling." He heads straight to the kitchen and begins making us lunch. He unpacks a loaf of bread, tomatoes, cucumbers, as well as a handful of other things grown in the garden.

I walk to the kitchen and lean my arms on the counter. I like watching Peter work, watching the way his muscles flex. Even the simplest movements, like making an avocado sandwich, are beautiful because of him. "What have you been up to today?"

"The girls found another creature today. A duck-like bird with feathers of orange and purple coloring mixed in with the usual brown and white. It's extraordinary." He slides the plate between us and takes one half of the sandwich. "I haven't seen one since I first came to the island."

"When was that, Peter?" I pry, trying to learn something about him. I've been an open book, answering every stupid thing he's asked, while I've been stonewalled. "You don't talk about the past."

"Because it's better left there."

"Right." I drop my half eaten sandwich on the plate and leave him in the kitchen. I've had enough. We haven't talked about what *this* is, but fuck buddies don't play house. If that's all we were, he would be eating my ass right now, not my sandwich. I walk to my room and slip on my shoes.

"Where are you going?" he asks when I open the door.

"Anywhere but here." I hesitate when I reach the wooden bridge. I haven't crossed one of these on my own in days. My legs shake but I need to make it to one of the other treehouses, any other tree house in this stupid web, to reach a ladder. I don't know where I'm going from there. I don't care either. I just need to get out of that treehouse.

Step by terrifying step I cross the first bridge. Peter follows, staying annoyingly close, barely a step behind, spotting my every move. I glance behind me, his hands are out, ready to catch me if I fall. I want to be mad, I was trying to get away from him, but I'm glad he's there.

"Look at you." Peter beams when we're on the ground. "Conquering your fears."

My heart is racing, but I feel good. Do I want to do that again? No, but at least I know I can make it on my own. "I didn't need your help back there."

"I know, but as long as your heart is beating I will be there whether you need me or not."

"And what if it doesn't? What happens then, Peter? Will I become one of The Lost, forever stuck on this island?"

I don't want the answer. I've come too close to dying too many times. It occurs to me that in both instances he was there. It pisses me off as I realize he could have been finishing what he started the other day. All of this was always his fault, everything I've been through both good and bad has been because he dragged me here.

"What will you do when you finally kill me? That's why you brought me to Neverland, isn't it? To finish what you started."

"Wednesday." Peter's eyes widen in shock. His head shakes back and forth, but I'm not sure I believe it's anything more than a show. "I pushed you off that boat in Florida, but you were never in danger of dying." He reaches for me but I pull away. I can't stand the thought of him touching me right now.

"You're lying."

Peter's brows draw together. He's quiet, likely trying to come up with another lie, but I'm not falling for his tricks anymore. I was stupid to trust him so blindly.

Maybe Peter didn't want me dead this time, but he certainly wanted me away from Cass. Damn that jealous prick. His plan worked.

I glance around looking for somewhere to stomp off to. I don't care if I'm being childish. But he'll follow me everywhere I go. *Almost everywhere.*

"I can prove it," Peter says, his voice jumping with emotion. "I can prove I never wanted to hurt you."

"How?"

"I need you to trust me. One more time." He drops to his knees and hugs my legs. "Please," he begs. "If you truly believe I wanted you dead after this, I promise I'll take you home."

"Today." It's not a question. I refuse to stay a minute longer than I have to. If Peter won't honor his word, there's a pirate in the cove waiting for me. Fucking him is no different than when I slept with Cass. I'll spread my legs one more time if it means getting home and away from this beautiful psychopath.

He nods. "Today."

"Fine. What do you need me to do?"

CHAPTER 32
Wednesday

"How much further?" I pant as we climb over a set of boulders somewhere in the heart of the island.

"Almost there, Darling." He's told me the same un-reassuring sentence four times in the last I don't know how many minutes. It lost its conviction a while ago.

My muscles protest every movement, strained from being contorted into positions they've never seen before. My hands are sweaty, fingers swollen and tingly. My chest burns, lactic acid seeping into each breath.

I hear the sound of rushing water before I see it. Panic slices through me. He doesn't honestly think I'm going to swim with him again?

Peter doesn't give me a passing glance. He ducks his head and continues up the terrain. I follow, two feet behind in case I need a running start. Eventually the thicket thins into a clearing. The grass before us is limited, spreading until there is no more room to roam.

Peter strides to the edge of the cliff. He stares down at the water cascading along the side of the mountain, falling in beautiful shades of white and blue.

I follow him but keep a safe distance. The sight is glorious, unlike anything I've ever seen, but I don't know what it has to do with Peter's truths.

Peter climbs the boulders to our left and sits on the highest one's edge, his legs dangling over. "Tell me about Neverland."

"What do you mean?" I inch closer. The spray of the water blowing upwards in the breeze is refreshing. I sit beside him, my stupid heart silencing the cynic in me that warns I'm in danger...again.

"I'm not an idiot, Darling. I know you found the book." He stares off at the horizon. From here we can see the forest cascading down the mountain to the beach and the endless ocean around us. "Tell me what you think you know about me and my island."

"Neverland is a place where you don't grow up." I tell him the story I learned as a child, about pirates who waged a war with him for no reason and the children he stole in the middle of the night. I talk about Tinkerbell and how her pixie dust mixed with happy thoughts makes everyone fly. My smile grows with each word. I love the tale, probably more than Tyle claims to. For her it was something else to take, but for me it was a story of infinite possibilities.

Peter is quiet as I finish my tale. He's got that far away look again, one that makes me wonder which memory he's lost in. "I fell in love with Wendy the moment I met her. She was beautiful, and kind, and... just..." He shakes his head, whispering, "More."

His lips lift into a sad smile. "But she was to marry my brother, James and as much as I hated it, there was nothing I could do."

I touch his arm, knowing how much it hurts to lose someone you love to a sibling. I wonder if James was like Tyle and stole Wendy maliciously, or if it was beyond his control. "I'm sorry."

"My father knew I loved Wendy and he still gave her to him. Wendy was a good wife. She was faithful even when I wished I could convince her otherwise." He lays back on the grass and tucks an arm behind his head. "She used to tell their boys, Michael and John, stories of an island filled with magic. She was a wonderful storyteller."

"You named Neverland after her."

He nods. "James thought it would be fun to charter a ship and search for her mysterious island. He planned to take the boys to any ol' piece of land and give them an adventure, but a storm came. Our ship fell into a whirlpool. I don't know what happened after that. All I know is we woke up on the shore, James, Wendy, some of the crew, and I. Everyone else was lost at sea."

"Oh, Peter." I can't imagine the pain he must have felt losing his nephews. I lost a cat once, Blue, and it destroyed me. He was my person, the other half of me for seven years of my life. My family didn't understand the pain it caused but I felt like I had lost a piece of myself. I can't imagine what losing a child you love feels like.

"The shit thing is, this island was everything Wendy described. The boys would have loved it. Especially the Faeries."

"Tinkerbell."

"Bell was one of the three on the island and the most underestimated. She was beautiful and free spirited, but evil. She was infatuated with James from the moment she laid eyes on him." Peter turns his head to look at me. He reaches out and touches one of my curls. "They aren't capable of love. They are obsessive and compulsive and will do anything to get what they want. Which is how we got ourselves into the mess we're in."

"Tink tried to kill Wendy. Didn't she?"

He twists my locks between one finger and the next. "I made a deal with the fae to save her life. My soul for hers, under the premise that I thought we would be together, but they took her away."

"Back to the land of the living."

"I always knew you were smart." Peter stands. He walks to the edge of the rock and tucks his hands in his pockets. "I didn't realize what I'd done when I made that deal. It's my fault The Lost are trapped in Neverland. I didn't know the fae would take every soul they touched. I thought they just wanted mine."

"It doesn't make sense." I touch his elbow. He looks down at my hand, then up at me. "How is their eternal damnation your fault? You didn't bring them here." Unlike me.

"It doesn't matter." He threads his fingers through my hair and touches his forehead to mine. "All that matters is that you're here. You *are* Wendy. Her soul brought back to life, reunited with mine. That's why this bond between us is so strong. You were only ever meant to be with me, Wednesday. You're my mate in every sense of the word."

I arch my back to put space between us. "Peter, that's crazy. You can't honestly think I'm your dead sister-in-law."

"Oh, Darling. But you are. Which is why I'd never risk your life, it's too valuable. Your return to Neverland means the curse is breaking. The souls can go home and we can be together again."

"I don't believe you. Take me home, Peter. You promised you would." I look up into his eyes. Emotion clogs my throat. "Please."

"Oh, Darling." Peter wraps his fingers around my neck and pulls my mouth to his. He kisses me and even though I want to fight it, my body melts into his. It falls under his spell and my lips spread right as he shoves me off the ledge.

CHAPTER 33
Wednesday

I'm going to kill him!

I don't bother screaming. I'm too mad. I should have known he would do something twisted. Afterall, he is Peter Pan, the conniving, trickster the stories are based off of, if I believe him.

I do believe him.

I believe everything he said, down to the notion that he never meant to put my life in danger. He wasn't the one to poison me on the beach.

The revelation is almost as startling as realizing I'm no longer being assaulted by wind. Strong arms hold me tight against a warm body. I close my eyes, letting his scent fill my lungs. I'm still pissed but as we float to the ground with the elegance of a feather I'm no longer afraid.

Peter sets me on my feet and steps back, an apologetic lift of his lips. He tucks his hands in his pockets and shrugs. "I'm sorry."

"You idiot!" I smack him. He takes my hit, his eyes steadily on me, filled with regret. There's a red mark on his cheek but it's not enough. I'm still pissed, filled with adrenaline from falling and so I shove his chest. "You could have killed me. Again."

"But I didn't."

"Is that supposed to make everything better?" Livid, I draw back to hit him again. He raises his arms defensively. His hands close around my wrists, restraining but not hurting me. "Take me home, Peter. You promised you would."

His face blanches as the fear that his trick might not have worked. I wish it hadn't.

"No," he says, his voice steady with authority.

"Fuck you, Peter." I yank my arms and he lets me go freely. I walk away from him with no clear direction as to where I am or where I'm going.

A thread in my chest tightens. Peter may be my soulmate and I may have loved him in another life but he doesn't deserve that love. I hope this wasn't how he treated Wendy because if so, I'm ashamed of my past self.

"Wednesday," he pleads, running after me. "I love you. I fell in love with you the moment I laid eyes on you, both in this lifetime and the last. Please...just..."

"No!" I spin on my heels to face him. Peter stops where he is, giving me some semblance of space but it's not enough. "You cut me."

I watch his gaze roam over my body, looking for a wound he can't see. My pain is every bit physical as it is emotional but the source is deep.

I place my hand over my heart, anger burning into tears I don't want to shed. "In here. I trusted you time and time again, and all you do is break that trust. I believe you when you say we're soulmates, and I believe that you don't want me dead, but you have a lot to learn about what it means to love someone. This..." I gesture to the island and everything that's conspired between us. "This isn't love. It's an obsession."

My words hit their target.

Peter lets me go without trying to stop or follow me.

I walk to the side of Neverpeek and follow the mountain's jagged terrain. I need space to sort through my emotions.

I feel too much.

Falling in love with Peter took a lifetime I don't remember living and yet the ache to be with him is as strong as if the experiences were my own. I need time to decide what I want to do with these feelings somewhere I won't be badgered by The Lost, stalked by Peter, or guilted by Cass.

I find a familiar rock formation and feel relief. I know one place Peter's shadow won't go. Someplace that'll buy me time with someone I should probably see.

CHAPTER 34
Wednesday

"Another round," I tell the man behind the bar.

He narrows his eyes on me but refills my cup for the third time. I don't have money to pay, and I think he suspects, but this is the same bar I stumbled into last week. James found me then and swore all I had to do was step back into Harper's Edge and he'd find me again.

I'm counting on him to keep his word.

And to pay my tab.

The brown liquid I ordered burns as it goes down my throat. It's not as potent as the stuff James bought me or as fast acting as the faery wine, but it's good. With each cup it stings less and I'm able to push aside my conversation with Peter that much more.

I take a swallow, then hold the mug in both hands, my thoughts torn. My goal this whole time has been to go home and Peter has kept that from happening.

Although, if I'm being honest, my original plan didn't work out like I'd hoped. I won't deny that I enjoyed sleeping with Cass and didn't give finding a way home my all, but Peter is one-hundred percent to blame for my current stalemate.

My thoughts teeter again and I'm back to my same internal debate. Every time I make up my mind that I'm leaving, there's a tug on the string that wraps around my heart. As crazy as it sounds, a small part of me doesn't want to say goodbye.

People spend their whole lives searching for the person they're meant to be with and I can't deny that I've found mine. I can't help but wonder if I'll regret walking away without giving us a fair chance. By Peter's wonky time logic, I've been missing for months. What harm could come from staying a few more days?

There's also the nagging thought of would he even let me go? I'd almost bet that he would track me down again. The thought, or perhaps the alcohol, lifts my lips. I would love to see him court me in my world.

I sit on my stool before the bar and think about what dating Peter would be like. We could share so many firsts together. I could take him to my favorite restaurant, show him what a movie theater is. We could stroll through the parks and he could call to the birds and I'd bet they'd swoop down to hear his song because he *is* Peter Pan.

I take another swallow of my drink, half wondering how it's nearly empty, but not caring enough to dwell on it.

"You're a sight for sore eyes." Cass slides onto the stool next to me and taps the bar top. A cup, twin to mine, is set before him, the same frothy brown drink inside.

"Eyes work two ways, mister." I point my fingers at my eyes and then his. I hold my serious face as long as possible but a hiccup ruins it.

Cass grins and I remember that was the first thing I noticed about him, gorgeous body aside. He was always so happy, truly, deeply, happy. I draw my brows together at his smile. It doesn't seem genuine.

"I tried to see you. We all did." He turns to face me and crosses his ankle over his knee. "Peter wouldn't let anyone in."

"Oh." That sounds like my Peter. So controlling. "And here I thought you didn't like me anymore."

I reach over and squeeze Cass's arm. He covers my hand with his, his touch colder than I remember. "I told you, beautiful, you shine too bright for the world. I could never gaze upon you with anything but wonder."

"Awwe. There's my riddler again." I suck in a breath. My bladder screams at me that it has to pee. It does that when I drink, gives me no notice before sending those annoying warning tingles to my belly. "I've got to find a bathroom."

He points to the corner of the bar. "I'll be here when you get back."

I tap his shoulder as I pass and run across the room. I make it to the toilet with just enough time to pull down my shorts. Peeing feels like heaven, the second best feeling to an orgasm. I stare at myself in the mirror as I wash my hands. I have to tell Cass about me and Peter.

143

If I were to leave Neverland tomorrow, my secret would haunt me and I don't like living with ghosts.

"I'm back." I slide onto my stool again.

Cass is on his second cup and mine has been refilled. I thank him and cheers our glasses together. I don't think I've ever seen Cass have more than one drink in the time we've been together. I nurse my glass as he finishes his and asks for a third.

"Are you okay?"

"Oh, beautiful, I'm far from it." He frowns and stares at the cream-colored froth. "Can I ask you a question?"

"Sure. What do you want to know?"

"Why him?"

I don't feel so good anymore. The alcohol I've drank turns to lead in my stomach. "I wanted to tell you."

Cass's lips quirk into a heartbroken smile. He nods and I think the question was based on suspicion more than knowledge. "I had a plan, you know. One I worked on for the equivalent of centuries if I were to live in your world."

"To do what?"

To take my home back." He drops his head. There's so much disappointment and longing in his tone.

I feel every word because I know what that pain is like. I want to go home so bad it hurts. I reach out and touch his arm.

A sharp pain pushes behind my eye, like a migraine hitting. I blink it back and try to comfort my friend. I'd like to think despite the way we ended that we are friends. "I'm sorry, Cass. Is there anything I can do?"

"Oh, beautiful. You already have." His face lifts into a smirk that makes my skin crawl. "You've already done more than you realize. I never stood a chance against Pan until you came."

"You," I whisper, my eyes widening in disbelief. I let my guard down and gave myself to him on so many levels, to the point that I would haveI trusted him with my life. It's a slap in the face. "It was you."

I pull my hand back and the movement sends the room spinning. I haven't drank enough to be feeling this disorientated. Something is wrong with me, again, and I know he's the reason.

"I don't know how you managed to survive the hemlock I laced your drink with, but I'm glad you did."

I press my palm to head, trying to stay the throb pulsating behind my eyes. It's horrible, making me light and sound sensitive.

"Turns out, Pan's magic is weaker when you're alive." Cass brushes his fingers across my cheek. I flinch, or try to but my reaction is delayed and not as impactful as I'd hoped. "The funny thing about magic, it's tied to your life. The more you use, the quicker it depletes you. Unless, of course, you're Peter. His powers were always a mystery to me. His shadow could do whatever it wanted and it never affected him. Until you. You tied Peter's magic to him and all I need to do is wear him down. Neverland was supposed to be mine. Now it will be."

"Get away from me, Cass."

"You'll be singing a different tune when the nightshade kicks in. In large doses it's fatal but the amount I gave you should only knock you out." He leans close and I can smell the magic on him. I never knew what the scent was before but I understand now; another truth gifted I didn't realize I needed. "Do you think Peter will cross the galaxies to find you?" He pauses, letting me process that I'm going to be taken somewhere against my will. Again. "I hope he does."

I stand and try to run away but my legs are shaky underneath me. Cass doesn't bother to follow as I try to flee. He watches, knowing my time is running out.

Unable to fully control myself, I bump into a table and spill someone's drink. "Sorry."

Their face has a halo of light around it. Everything is blurry and getting harder to see. My body harder to control.

Firm hands grab my shoulders. I look up, unable to recognize the face, their features blobs of black and tan and red, but I recognize his scent. A familiar hint of earth, sage, and bad decisions. As much as I hate that I'm forced to trust him, I'm glad he's here.

"What happened?" Peter asks, his voice dripping with concern. His hands shake and I wonder if it's his body twitching or mine. I hope it's mine because I can feel the air around us trembling.

"Help me."

. . .

To be continued...

LOOKING FOR MORE?

Sign up to my newsletter for an exclusive subscriber only bonus chapter from Peter's perspective.

Click Here

BAILEY'S OTHER BOOKS

ROMANCE NOVELS UNDER THE NAME BAILEY B

UNEXPECTED

BAILEY B.

Asher Anderson is a dick.

We aren't friends, so when he seeks me out in the cafeteria on the worst day of my life, I'm suspicious. When he tells Liam Heiter that we'er dating, which couldn't be farther from the truth, I want to kill him.

Until I see Liam's reaction.

Liam—my best friend, the guy who crushed every hope of us *officially* being together—is jealous. He has never looked at me this way and I love it.

So, I play along.

Maybe watching me with someone else will make Liam suffer like I have the past four years. And maybe, just maybe, he'll come to his senses and realize we belong together.

It's not like I actually *like* Asher. At best, I tolerate him.

What's the worst that can happen?

CHAPTER 1

Maggie Mills, my best friend since freshman year, hip bumps me then leans against the cold metal lockers that line B-hallway of Ridgewater High School. Her lips pull down into a frown, disapproving dark eyes narrowed into slits. "You're staring again."

I force a smile and close my locker door, forgetting the chemistry notes I opened it for. I leave the spiral bound paper inside, tucked between my English Lit book and my Pre-Calc folder. Grabbing them now will affirm Maggie's suspicion that I was indeed staring at Liam Heiter and press play on her broken record of disapprobation. "Was not."

Maggie turns her head to me, ruby red lips pressed into a thin line. She's quiet, watching me scrutinize the expression that's clear as day on her face. Whatever she's about to say, I'm not gonna like it. "Did you hear? Liam asked Corah to prom. Seems like things are getting serious between them."

I choke on air that lodges itself in my throat but twist the sound into a meager laugh. Liam Heiter—my other best friend, the one I've known since diaper days—doesn't do serious. After a month, two tops, he breaks things off because those girls can't offer him what I can. Family. History. Love without strings.

I twist the cap off of my water and take a sip to settle my nerves. Corah Raymond is no different than any other girl who has tried to settle Liam down. She's the flavor of the moment, whereas what Liam and I have goes beyond words. Our relationship has built every year we've been together, blossoming from a booming friendship into an all consuming fire.

"There's only one way to find out if the rumors are true." I toss my water bottle at Maggie and pull my phone out of my back pocket.

I talk a good game, pretending that watching Liam with every girl who bats her eyes in his direction doesn't bother me when, really, it does. Even knowing he and I are endgame, the few weeks his arms wrap around anyone else is nothing shy of hell. I live for the moments he's single, when we can be together.

"Lee." I beam at the nickname I've used since before I could form real words. The nickname no one else is allowed to utter. I hold my phone up, pretending to record our conversation for the school paper I don't actually write for. I take pictures that never get used, but the extracurricular looked good on my college applications. "Comment for the paper?"

Liam lifts one corner of his lips into a lopsided grin. My heart flutters as his emerald eyes lock onto my boring browns. High school has been his playground because, not only does his personality demand attention, his good looks attract it.

While Liam grew into a walking god of a man the past few years, I, unfortunately, stayed the same lanky beanpole I've been since middle school.

My boobs came in and filled a smaller than average bra in the seventh grade but they forgot they were supposed to keep growing; my butt has just enough cushion not to hurt the chair; and my shoulder-length hair hasn't figured out that when I spend forty-five minutes straightening, blow-drying, and sticking every product known to man in it, it's supposed to stay pretty. I blame the Florida heat for that last one.

Most days I look like a pubescent boy who stuck his finger in a light socket. At least, that's what the popular girls tell me. The same popular girls who are currently glaring, wordlessly reminding me that I am not worthy of breathing the same air as them.

"Only for you," he declares. *Always for me.*

"Elaine," Corah purrs with a chastising smile.

I hate her. I hate her perfect hair and toned body. I hate how Liam's muscles flex beneath the sleeve of his shirt when he pulls her close. Most of all, I hate that she's at his side while I'm three feet away trying to remind her, and me, that I am important.

"Football season is over. What could the paper possibly need to know about my Lee Lee?" Corah pinches Liam's chin between her fingers and pulls his lips to hers. The kiss, while quick, is strategic. A show of power on her part. I may be reminding Corah that I was here first, but she's not going to let me forget that, for the time being, he's all hers.

My stomach twists inside itself. I usually avoid Liam when he's got a girlfriend, keeping our interactions to lunch and the confines of my bedroom. Watching him with someone else is too painful. And yet, here I am. *Keep it together, Lainey.* "Rumor has it, you two are going to prom together. Tell me how that happened."

Liam pulls back from Corah's embrace and narrows his ember eyes on me. He knows this conversation won't make it into the paper. This is for me. Sure, I could have texted to ask my burning questions, but I want to hear the truth straight from the horse's mouth. Most importantly, I want to hear that Maggie is wrong.

"I asked. She said yes."

"Don't be modest, Lee Lee." Corah giggles. She leans into him and presses her perfectly manicured fingers against his chest. Corah may be dense, but she is not stupid. She intentionally digs her knife deeper into my wounds, pouring salt with each detail I've yet to hear. "If the people want to know, let's tell them."

Corah pauses, waiting for Liam to spill the beans. When he doesn't, she is more than happy to do it for him. "It was last Saturday. Lee Lee picked me up for our night on the town like he always does, but I immediately knew something was off. He was too quiet in the car and he would barely hold my hand. When he pulled into Riverside, my gut twisted because everyone knows that is his breakup spot."

I stare at Liam, my eyebrows nearly kissing my hairline. Riverside Park is our special place and has been ever since we were kids. Every relationship he's been in has ended there because he was thinking about me.

Coming back to me.

I wait for some silent explanation as to why Liam would bring *her* there, of all places, but he breaks eye contact with me to stare at the floor.

"And when Lee Lee took me to the playground, I thought for sure we were done," Corah continues. "I followed him out of the car, practically tripping over my feet because my eyes were blurry with tears. And you know what he said to me?"

"What?" Please tell me, because I can't fathom why he would taint what's ours with this trash.

Corah looks up at Liam, doe-eyed, and smiles. "He said it was on the playground that he first fell in love."

Her voice fades into the background. My pulse thunders through my body with loud, almost deafening thrums. It takes every ounce of willpower I have not to run and jump into his arms but I can't do that because no one knows about Liam and me. We chose to keep our unorthodox relationship a secret so high school doesn't ruin it. Things between us aren't ideal and, to keep appearances, Liam has to date. I could see other people too, but it's easier if I don't.

I chew on the inside of my cheek and silently plead to the universe for Liam to look at me. He needs to understand that I love him too. I don't care if it took three years of secretly pining after him and another five years of him sneaking through my window late at night for us to get here, but his gaze is glued to the ground.

"That's why Liam took me there, because that silly playground was where he found his first love, and he thinks I might be his last." Corah clasps her hands over her heart, feigning happy tears.

Dark spots cloud my vision but, at the moment, they are better than tears because my internal compass is spinning in circles and I'm a ball of emotions. I want to scream. I want to yank Corah by the hair out of Liam's arms and then, of course, I want to cry.

Somehow I manage to force it all down—the humiliation, the self-pity, the tears, and most of all, the anger— and make myself smile again.

"I know what you're thinking," Corah beams.

No. I highly doubt she does. If she did, she wouldn't be hanging on the arm of the man I love. Gloating. She would be running, because the things I want to do to her, to both of them, aren't legal in fifty states.

"It wasn't a big, fancy promposal, but I didn't need anything glamorous. The way Lee Lee asked, it came from the heart and that's what matters most." Corah snuggles into Liam's side and looks up at him like the sun rises and sets because he exists.

I know it does in my world. I shiver, feeling a chill as the actual sun dips behind a cloud. Ironic considering we're inside and its rays barely shine through a nearby window. Still, I feel the darkness nonetheless.

"You must have been thrilled." I force the words out, dying a little with each syllable.

Liam finally lifts his emerald gaze to meet mine. There's no remorse in his expression. No regret for breaking my heart into unmendable pieces. What I find is worse.

Pity.

The bell rings and, for once, I couldn't be more grateful there are only two and a half minutes between classes. If I have to stand here any longer pretending to be happy for these two, I might crack.

"We should go," Liam says, leading both him and Corah towards A-hall. The same hallway I should be going to, but I can't seem to make my feet move. I can't bring myself to walk behind them and watch their happiness. Their circle of friends follow like peasants, eager for the attention of the king and his new queen. A few steps down the hallway, Liam looks over his shoulder at me. "See you tonight."

"Are you okay?" Maggie asks once Liam has turned down the hall-way. Her hand reaches out and I watch her fingers touch my arm. I feel nothing. My mind is too busy keeping my head above the swell of tears and holding onto a smile to process anything else.

"Yeah." I don't sound like myself. My voice is strained, cracking with emotion while coming out an octave higher than normal. "I just need a minute."

Maggie's perfectly plucked eyebrows knit together. Everything she wants to say is written on her face.

Don't let that jerk get to you. He never deserved your heart. You'll get through this. Everything will be okay.

But she keeps it all to herself. "Alright. I have my extra credit thing with Mr. Alverson today, but I'll try to be done in time for lunch." She pauses, studying me a little longer. "Are you sure you're okay?"

I nod, my lips stretched tight across my face. The smile couldn't be faker, but Maggie doesn't press the issue.

After what feels like an eternity, she sighs and says, "Okay, sweetie. I'll see you later, but text me if you need me."

"Will do."

The moment she rounds the corner of B-hall, the dam of tears I was holding together with scotch tape and band-aids cracks. The world around me blurs into starbursts of light as liquid pain trails down my cheeks.

I run into the nearest bathroom and press my back against the wall. I squeeze my eyes shut, forcing myself to take slow, steady breaths

—a tactic my therapist taught me back in middle school when my social phobia controlled my life. *Deep breath in. And let it out. One. Two. Three. Four. Five.* It takes a few cycles for the pressure in my chest to decrease and the waterworks to dry up, but eventually I start to feel better.

A toilet flushes in a nearby stall and the nervous needles under my skin spring back to life. I can't bring myself to look at who is here and see either a smug smile or a look of pity from someone who thinks they know what has happened. I keep my eyes closed, using eight-year-old logic of, *if I can't see you, you can't see me.* I know that's not how the world works, but it makes me feel better.

The lock on the stall door slides open, metal scraping inside itself. Heavy footfalls take one step, and then two, and then stop. Silence eats away at my resolve to stay strong and keep my eyes closed. After the slowest five seconds of my life, I hear, "You look like shit."

You've got to be kidding me!

My eyes snap open at the deep rumble that is uniquely Asher Anderson's. He's got this smoked-a pack-a-day rasp, paired with knee-knocking baritone pitch. If Snow White and the Prince ever had a son, it would be him. With hair as dark as a starless sky and moon kissed skin, the contrast is striking. But then you add in his eyes, a unique shade of amethyst that looks too perfect to be real. The girls around here all but melt at the sight of him. Liam may be the shining king of the school, but Asher is the prince wearing a crown of thorns.

Asher crosses the bathroom to wash his hands in the sink, shaking loose water droplets into the porcelain bowl when he's done, never breaking eye contact. Not even when he reaches for a paper towel from the dispenser.

"Get out!" I scream, unable to take his patronizing stare any longer. This is the girl's bathroom for Christ's sake. Is this man so heartless as to beat me here just to inflict more pain on my already bleeding heart?

Wouldn't put it past him.

I've known Asher all my life. Our parents—mine, Liam's, and Asher's mom—used to be friends. I still remember the stories my mother would tell about how excited she was for all of them to be pregnant around the same time. We were a heartbeat away from being a B-rated version of the sitcom *Friends* if they'd all had kids.

Until one day when everything imploded.

As for Asher and I, we drifted apart in the sixth grade after he ridiculed me for getting my first period. As if I wasn't embarrassed enough to find a puddle of red when I stood to jump into the pool, Asher let everyone at that birthday party know what happened. He even went as far as calling me shark bait the rest of the year. Liam thought it was hilarious. I wanted to die.

"Perhaps I should say the same to you." Asher chuckles and leans his ass against the sink, crossing his long, muscular arms.

My jaw drops. This is my bathroom. He... My train of thought is lost as I take in my surroundings. The girl's bathroom has more than two stalls and it doesn't have urinals.

No. No. No! I cover my face with my hands, mortified. *Could today get any worse?*

"It's cool," Asher guffaws. "No one will walk in on us if that's what you're worried about. Besides, it looks like you need a moment."

I let my hands fall to my sides, shoulders rolling forward. I know Asher's sympathy will come with a price, but I do need a minute's peace. I don't know how I'm going to make it through lunch and my next three classes. Everyone is talking about prom and now all I'll be able to think about is Liam and his stupid promposal. "It's girl shit. I'm fine."

"You don't look fine." Asher steps closer, crossing the tiny bathroom in only three strides.

I turn my head and stare at a phone number someone scribed onto one of the stalls. I hate looking at Asher. He makes my stomach jump and my heart flutter at the same time. One a feeling of irritation. The other... not going there.

Asher tucks his knuckle under my chin and lifts, forcing my gaze back to him. "You look like Liam stomped all over your heart. Again."

I jerk my chin free of his grasp and lean back against the wall. I'd rather touch the cream-colored tiles with all its grimy germs than him. I hate him. I don't hate him. I don't know how I feel about Asher. Things between us are... complicated. Always have been.

"You don't know what you're talking about."

"Don't I though?" Asher chuckles again. The dude laughs a lot, only it never sounds happy. There's always a hidden layer of darkness or sorrow or something straight up evil in it.

Asher steps back and grabs the door's handle. He tugs it open and steps out, leaving me alone in the boy's bathroom. I take a second to gather my thoughts, grateful to finally be alone.

I shake my head, irritated that he thinks he knows me. Knows what I'm feeling. Asher doesn't know jack shit about having a broken heart. He's the heartbreaker, just like Liam, leaving a trail of tears wherever he goes.

FALLING FOR YOU

Read on Amazon

Josh

I met the girl of my dreams in a church parking lot while my best friend was having sex in my truck. Her name was Layla and she was trying her hardest to ignore me, and them, from two parking spaces over. I swear, I've never seen someone so beautiful in my life. I've also never struggled to get the girl, but for some reason my foot and my mouth became friends that night in the worst of ways. Cheesy pick up line, that failed? Check. Inability to form coherent sentences? Check.

Ego crushing let down? Yup. That happened too. I can't put my finger on it, but there's something about Layla that sucks me in. I need to get to know her. Spend time with her. Make her mine. Who knows, maybe she will be the one to finally settle me down. That is, if I can convince her to give me the time of day.

Layla

Everything about Joshua Thomas screams, run away. His sharp jaw. Those vibrant eyes. Lush lips that have probably tasted every girl in this tiny town. I know better than to give him a chance, but knowing what I should do and listening are two different things. He makes my heart flutter in ways I thought only possible in Hallmark movies. He makes my legs shake from one look. I resisted him once. I don't know if I can do it again.

Sneak Peek

PROLOGUE

Layla

A chill slithers through me as I look out the window from my seat in row 23A. Our pilot circles the runway, waiting for the go-ahead from the control tower to launch us into the sky. Tonight's flight is relatively short but it's on an older plane, so there's no movie.

To add to my bad luck, there's no internet up in the clouds, which means the new books I wanted to read on my Kindle app are useless. I should have downloaded them before takeoff or bought a magazine at the kiosk, but because of my lack of planning I'm stuck on an almost two hour flight with nothing but my thoughts.

One thought in particular won't leave me alone: Why am I going back?

It's not the quietness of a small town or how the stars shine brighter away from the big city that draws me in. Nor is my return for the friends I left, because Hattie Reynolds is the only person to text me since I left.

What's pulling me back is what's kept me away for so long—Joshua Thomas—and it's not a matter of if I'll run into him, it's when, because Hattie's boyfriend, Landon Waters, is one of Josh's best friends.

I wrap my arms around my waist. As much as I've talked myself up to the possibility of running into Josh, I'm not ready to see him again.

Butterflies are throwing a party, dousing my insides with buckets of vomit that threaten to expel themselves into the tiny paper bag the airplane has provided for such occasions.

Do I love Josh?

No.

Yes.

I'm not sure.

Love is a fickle word with expectations and the possibility of a future attached to it. All I know is I've never felt a pull to be near someone like I do when I'm with him, and a part of me I didn't know existed broke when I left.

So, that brings me back to my original question. Why come back? Why subject myself to the pain and the embarrassment of looking like an idiot to him and the people I thought were my friends?

The easy answer? Because I am a fool.

What was it Elvis said? Only fools fall in love? Or perhaps it's that they rush in? I don't know. However the saying goes, I did both—rushed into a relationship and fell too hard.

I slide the window shade up and notice our pilot circling the landing strip. I've done it again, gotten lost in my thoughts while time races away from me. I've been doing that a lot since moving back to Georgia. Losing time.

Fifteen minutes later, the plane touches down and I'm allowed to disembark. I grab my rolling carry-on bag and my backpack from the overhead compartment, then shuffle my way through the sea of bodies in the terminal.

After a quick chat with the car rental company, and a nerve-racking two hour drive, I finally make it to the yellow one-bedroom cottage that Hattie and Landon call home. No one pays me any attention as I cross the grassy knoll beside the house. A cruel reminder that these people were never really my friends.

I take a deep breath, hoping it will settle my nerves and head for the kitchen. Tonight isn't a night I want to tackle sober.

The front door is open, so I let myself in. Dozens of empty bottles line the cabinet tops like trophies. It's stupid, if you ask me, because I'd bet a hundred dollars he can't remember anything about the parties he drank them at.

I open the fridge, unsurprised to see it filled with White Claw, beer, and Jello shots. I grab a plastic container, filled with what I'm hoping is watermelon flavored Jello. I swipe my tongue around the inside edge, loosening the gelatinous goo, and swallow. Without giving myself time to change my mind, I reach in and grab a beer. I've never liked White Claw, it always reminded me of flavored seltzer water, but Hattie loves the stuff.

"Ahhhhh!" a girl screams from behind me.

I know that high-pitched squeal, but recognizing the sound doesn't stop me from jumping and hitting my head on the edge of the freezer door. I pop the top of my can, then rub the sore spot with my free hand while I take my first sip of the night. I don't particularly like beer, but it hits faster than Jello.

Hattie runs into the kitchen, hands waving about like a madwoman, before throwing them around my neck. The sheer force of her embrace makes me stumble back against the fridge. I peel her blue tinged strands from my lipstick and force a laugh. While I'm happy to see Hattie, and for someone to be excited I'm here, I don't feel gleeful. My skin is crawling, my stomach is twisting, and I need her to let me go before I hyperventilate. "Good to see you too, Hattie."

"You have no idea how much I've missed you." She releases me as the world begins to spin out of focus. Like almost everyone else here, Hattie is drunk. Unsurprising, considering how late it is.

I bite my lip, wondering if I should have waited until morning to come by. I could have blamed missing her nineteenth birthday on a delayed flight, or something. Too bad I know myself. If I didn't come out tonight, I wouldn't have showed up at all.

Hattie grabs my hand and takes a step backward. "Two months is too long."

I allow her to lead me towards the living room. There are too many memories in the kitchen. Here. There. Everywhere. "How'd you know it was me?"

She plops onto the faded green cushion, one leg under her, the other off the side, and gives me a lopsided grin. "Please. I'd know that flat ass anywhere."

I can't help but laugh when she slaps me on the thigh. It feels good to be back, but it also feels different. Landon and Hattie's place has always been more like a home to me than my own, but tonight the air is thick.

I look around the tiny room. Nothing has physically changed, everything is the same as it was a few weeks ago, but there's still a shift.

Maybe it's me.

Maybe I'm different.

CHAPTER 1

Layla
1 year earlier

A dark haired girl in a pair of faded skinny jeans and a floral crop-top leans against an older style red Nissan Altima, probably waiting for me. She pops her gum, not bothering to glance up from her phone as my rental car's headlights paint her in yellow.

I park behind the Nissan and press the lock button on the keyfob out of habit. This neighborhood seems safe enough with its picket fences and solar powered street lights, but clicking the button again to unlock it is redundant.

The girl, I'm assuming to be Kelly Brewer, looks up, finally acknowledging my existence. "I take it you're Layla?"

I smile and try to look excited for tonight. If I play my cards right, Kelly will think her mom and my aunt have set us up on a blind-friend-date because I'm visiting from Georgia, lame, and have no life. She doesn't need to know that I've been sent as insurance. If Kelly stays out of trouble tonight, her mom has promised to donate to Aunt Tricia's latest fundraiser.

My job is to make sure she doesn't get arrested or pregnant, or do anything to jeopardize the twenty-thousand dollar check coming our way on Sunday. But hanging out with strangers for the night, doing god-knows-what, is one hundred percent out of my comfort zone. I'm an introvert at heart, only going out when absolutely necessary, and this is my personal hell.

"You must be Kelly."

I extend my hand and let it hang in the air for a solid three seconds before dropping it back to my side. Kelly rolls her eyes and turns around while unlocking her car. "Let's go."

I pat my back pockets, double checking that I grabbed my phone. Satisfied that I have it, my driver's license, and my debit card, I walk around to the passenger side of the Nissan.

Kelly's door creaks as it opens. I force another smile, even though the woman has barely glanced at me, just in case she's embarrassed. By the looks of the inside of her car, I doubt she cares about the sound her door makes. The front seat is disgusting, covered in receipts, fast food bags—that I hope are empty—and gas station Slupree cups. I push everything in the seat onto the floorboard, then buckle up.

I suck in a breath and grin again. If not for the darkness blanketing us, Kelly would for sure see my shaking hands. Going solely off what my Aunt Tricia told me about Kelly—that her parents think she parties too much and might need rehab—I'd say there's a good chance we're going to some kind of social gathering. I just hope tonight isn't as much of a disaster as her car is.

Kelly turns her key in the ignition, then faces me, and wrinkles her nose. "Are you going to church?"

I tug the ends of the three-quarter sleeve pink sweater that covers my black tank top. I paired it with a pair of dark skinny jeans and ankle-high boots. I shake my head, thinking about how my parents would skin me alive if I went to Sunday service in something like this. "No."

"Coulda fooled me," Kelly scoffs, rolling her eyes again. She shifts the car into gear, but hesitates before pulling out of her driveway. "Just so we're clear, if anyone asks, I don't know you."

I tuck my lips between my teeth and nod, slightly relieved. Judging by the leather miniskirt and neon orange tube top Kelly's wearing, I'd say she's the kind of girl who craves attention. I could be wrong, but we'll see.

Me, I'm the blend into the background kind of girl. Pretending not to know Kelly, unless I'm in the confines of her car. "Sounds good to me."

***

Three parties, one McDonald's drive through run, a quick stop on the side of the road to pee, and we're finally headed back to Kelly's house.

I'm beyond ready. Back home, I'm not much of a partier. I go out every now and then when my parents force me to, but I don't think I've ever stayed out this late.

"I take it you lost that last round of beer pong?" I ask when Kelly gives up singing Katy Perry's "I Kissed A Girl" to plant a wet one on my cheek.

"I haven't won a game of beer pong since I was sixteen." Kelly throws her head between her legs and tosses one empty McDonald's cup after another behind her into the back seat. She sits up, her head finding the headrest with a thud. "I think I lost my phone."

I press my lips onto a line and fight a scowl. Kelly is a train wreck of epic proportions. Her flip-flop broke two parties ago, she's slept with three guys that I know of, and now she can't remember where she tucked her phone.

Do I think she needs rehab?

No, but if you look up hot mess in the dictionary, you'll find her picture.

"It's in your bra."

"Huh?" Kelly looks down, finally realizing the end of her bright pink iPhone case is visible between her massive chest and orange top. She squeals then laughs. "There it is!"

My aunt sure knows how to pick them.

"Hey, I know that truck!" Kelly pulls her phone from her shirt and squints at its backlight, somehow managing to find the number she's looking for. "Hey, sexy thing. What are you doing?"

Her high-pitched voice falters when the mystery man on the other end talks. I can't understand what he's saying, but I know what he wants. By the way Kelly is licking her lips, it seems like she's ready for round four. She hangs up and says, "Turn there."

"No. It's like two in the morning. I need to get you home so I can drive back to Orlando and go to bed."

"It's too late to drive back to your aunt's place. Just crash at my house tonight." Kelly folds her hands, prayer style. "Please."

Considering I have to go back to her house for my rental car anyway, staying with Kelly tonight doesn't sound like the worst idea. At least there I can sleep in. Aunt Tricia insists the whole house be up at five a.m, no matter what day of the week it is. "Fine."

Kelly shrieks and points at an upcoming streetlight. "There! Turn there!"

After more wrong turns than right, we eventually make it to an empty church parking lot, seconds before a truck pulls in. Kelly jumps out of the passenger seat before it can shift into park.

I watch her wait like a kid on Christmas for her newest conquest: a lanky blonde that is attractive, but not my type.

The guy holds his arms out and Kelly runs into them, jumping and latching her legs around his waist. He fuses his mouth to hers, carries her back to his truck, and lowers the tailgate.

I lean the seat of the Nissan back and close my eyes. The last thing I want to see is someone's white ass in the air, or any other body parts.

The car door opens again and I squeeze my lids tighter, casting out the overhead light's brightness. I sense a body next to me, but it doesn't smell like Kelly. It smells like whiskey, spices, and wood.

Peeling one eye open, I squint at the intruder. A black cowboy hat shadows most of the face that is looking at me, but the parts of him I can see are attractive. Strong arms. A tight button down shirt. And a pair of jeans that don't leave much to the imagination. I open both eyes and lift my head off the seat. The guy tips the front of his hat at me. I blush, not because I'm flattered, but because people don't do things like that where I'm from.

"Hey there." He has a thick, southern accent, too strong for a

Florida boy. I fight a smile as I sit my seat up. The passenger door closes and the overhead light goes out almost immediately, but the glow of the streetlamp is bright enough that I can somewhat make out his face. He leans forward, turns the music down, and says, "You're pretty."

I can't tell if the over annunciation is from that southern twang or if it's alcohol-induced. Either way, this guy's accent is sexy. I feel his eyes on me, waiting for the acknowledgement I refuse to give. I watch Mr. Cowboy shift from the corner of my eye. He leans forward, resting his elbows on his knees, hands clasped together.

What is he doing?

He sits up straight and leans closer until his warm whiskey breath tickles my cheeks. Heat climbs my neck at the thought of him kissing me. Not because I'm interested—I'm not—but I've only kissed one man. My ex, Ashley.

"I'm a bull rider."

I laugh and the guy's head cocks to the side. He didn't honestly expect that line to work. Did he? What tiny butterflies I may have felt about Mr. Cowboy maybe kissing me disappear. Kelly needs to hurry up and finish, because I need to get as far away from this loser as possible.

CHAPTER 2

Josh

Kelly is on Sam like white on rice before I can make it around the front of my truck. Sam would have fucked her right there in the parking lot, but that's not cool. Kelly may be easy, but she still deserves some semblance of privacy.

"Y'all wanna use my—"

They climb into the back before I can finish getting the words out. Shaking my head, I make my way over to Kelly's car. Knowing her, she left it unlocked and running for a quick get-in-get-out kind of thing.

Opening the passenger door, I have every intention of laying the seat back and closing my eyes. This ain't my first rodeo with those two; this little sexcapade could last a while.

The overhead light clicks on when the door opens and my breath catches in my chest. The most beautiful girl I've ever seen is sleeping in the driver's seat. Something inside of me shifts. The need to talk to this girl and make a good impression consumes me. She opens one eye and looks up. Realizing the light must have woken her, I tip my hat and slip in the passenger seat so the light can click off.

"Hey there." Fucking, hell. What am I, sixty? Who talks like this? Why can't I be normal and just say hi.

The girl doesn't say anything. She doesn't smile, but her gaze darts over to me a few times. Maybe I can save this. "You're pretty."

"Thanks." She looks out the window towards my truck.

I stare at her, waiting for her to look at me again. One second. Two seconds. Four seconds. Shit.

There's no other choice. I have to pull out my go-to line. It's a hook, line, and sinker every time. "I'm a bull rider."

It all starts with her eyes. They find me first, and then her head turns. A fraction of a second later, the corners of her mouth lift into a small but noticeable smirk.

There's a sweet satisfaction knowing that I've broken through her façade, but all I want is to taste those lips. I'd probably be useless for anything else tonight. Gotta love Jack Daniels.

I lean closer and her scent makes my head swim. Flashing my best smile, I say again, "I'm a bull rider."

The girl laughs and shakes her head. If I hadn't drank a fifth of whiskey, I might be offended, but I find her resistance endearing. Most of the girls around here throw themselves at me, but not this one. The fact that she doesn't want me makes me want her even more. One way or another, I will win her over.

She turns her head, bringing her gaze to mine. It's too dark to tell what color her eyes are but I bet they're beautiful. "I have a boyfriend."

"I don't see him here tonight." I reach my hand out and touch her cheek. I stare at her lips, unable to think about anything else. Most of the girls I screw around with taste like beer. I'd put money on it that this one doesn't. I'm guessing she'll taste like cherry because of the Chapstick in the center console.

The overhead light clicks on, blinding me. My eyes are slow to adjust but when they do, I open the passenger door, stand, and watch this chick cross the parking lot.

She pounds her fist against the side of my truck, a move that would have gotten her face beaten if she were a dude. "I swear to god, Kelly, if you aren't in your car in one minute, I'm leaving without you."

BEAUTIFULLY BROKEN

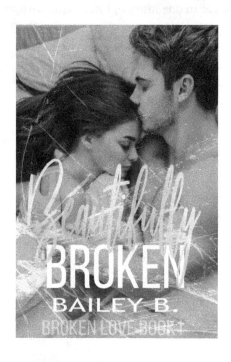

N ow Available
   Most people don't think about the day they'll die. They coast through life, blissfully unaware of how their time is ticking away. I wasn't like most people. I welcomed death, wanted her to take me away from the prison I called life, but she refused. I tried twice only to survive. And then, when I thought I had nothing left it came.

A reason to live.

. . .

Rex was a small, unexpected ray of light my world of darkness that blossomed into a beam of sunshine. I thought, maybe this was why Death didn't take me. Maybe she knew that if I held on a little longer things would turn around. But the third time Death came to my door wasn't by choice. Someone else brought her, and I fear this time she might take me.

Rex

Being the son of a country star sucks. My parents are never around, I move every year or so, and I have no real friends. Everyone around me has an agenda. Everyone except Piper Lovelace. I can't get that girl to notice me. Trust me I've tried.

Thankfully, fate stepped in and gave me the break I needed. I've got her attention, now I need her to give me a chance.

CHAPTER 1

PIPER

I'm the school slut. It's a title I wear, not proudly, but because it's what's expected of me. Everyone at St. A's High School knows my bio-mom's a whore—a real screw-you-for-money whore— that slept with the physics teacher last week.

Thank you, Facebook, for tagging me in that humiliating article.

Not.

Bio-mom was arrested for all of two seconds before making bail thanks to her pimp and the John she got caught with, he also happens to be my first period teacher this year. So, on top of the normal whispers spread about me on the daily, that mess is going around too.

It's fine.

I'm used to my name being in everyone's mouth. It's been that way since the third grade. Back then, people talked about my dirty nails, how skinny I was, and how my best friend was a boy. In high school, the daily gossip changed to where I moved to, what alleged drugs I was on, and eventually who I had spread my legs for. When the rumor started that I gave a killer blowjob for fifty bucks, no one doubted it. Why would they? I'm the girl with a whore for a mom. The girl from the wrong side of the tracks.

Literally.

There's the rich side of town where my classmates live, the good side, the tracks, and then *that* side. It's like the shadowy place in the *Lion King* Simba was warned to stay away from. Yeah...bio-mom lives there.

Anyway, not long after that rumor about me started, I figured what the hell. They say when life gives you lemons, make lemonade. I was given stupid, horny boys. So, I made money.

For the record, I've never actually touched anybody. At first, I turned everyone who approached me down. But there were a select few I eventually said yes to. The most selfish, conceited, disrespectful guys in our school got special treatment.

Underneath the shadows of the stadium bleachers, they dropped their pants. Exposed their less-than-exciting-junk to me. And then I kicked them straight in the balls. Those jerks fell to their knees, cursing my name while I took all the cash from their wallets. It was the perfect hustle.

Anyway, all of this is why I'm being stared down by Tad Parker. Captain of the baseball team, running back on the football team, and total tool. Bloodshot eyes narrow on my face, expecting a different answer to the question asked this morning.

"It's still a hard no, Tad." I stop walking and cross my arms.

While I'd love to take the pretty boy for all he's got, I'm trying to turn a new leaf and make the most of what's left of my senior year. I don't expect to fix my reputation, but I'm trying to change the way I see myself. Which means no more pretend illicit acts for money.

Tad rolls his bloodshot eyes and pulls a brown leather wallet, that probably costs as much as a year's tuition, from his back pocket. He thumbs through his cash, offering more twenties than I've held in my entire life. "Come on, Piper. I'll make it worth your while. Five hundred. Right now for five minutes in the bathroom."

Tad's a good looking guy, if you're into that classic blond-haired, blue-eyed, prince charming wannabe look with the attitude of Gaston.

He has no shortage of self-entitled princesses throwing themselves at him.

I shake my head and push his arm back. My checking account may be teetering on the edge of zero, but I'm not this desperate. "Why not hit up one of the JV cheerleaders. They'd jump at the chance to get tangled up with you. For free."

"Because they aren't Piper fucking Lovelace. Now come on." Tad's hand curls around my arm. He squeezes, pulling me towards the stadium bathrooms.

One Mississippi.

My airway constricts. Bats swarm in my stomach, threatening to bring up the vending machine cinnamon roll I had after fourth period. I absolutely detest being touched; it sets off a catalyst of reactions that steadily get worse. My one and only thought at this point is to make Tad let go.

I dig my heels into the ground and yank my arm back, but my efforts are useless. I try to pry his fingers off me, punch him, kick him in the leg. Nothing I do makes a difference. Tad's too strong. Even with my best attempt at a struggle, he drags me clear across the parking lot almost effortlessly.

Two Mississippi.

My hands tremble, sending vibrations up my arms and throughout my body. I need help. I hate asking for help almost as much as I hate being touched, but I don't have much choice. I look to my left and then my right, but there's no one in sight. No one to hear my screams. I try anyway, opening my mouth to yell, but nothing comes out. *This can't be happening.* I swallow the tiny bit of saliva in my bone dry throat and try again.

Nothing but air.

Beads of sweat drip down my neck as the feeling of impending doom lingers. The memory of a crooked grin I'll never forget flashes before my eyes, amping the intensity of my breakdown.

I spent a good part of this year in counseling to learn how to manage my panic attacks. Finding ways to keep everyone from noticing my freak outs. Tad makes me feel like I'm trapped, watching from the outside, as I lose all control.

Three Mississippi.

Logically I know it's been more than three seconds. It has to have been, but I'm stuck in a time warp. Everything happens at a snail slow pace yet lightning fast at the same time.

Tad pushes me against a wall near the entrance of the girl's bathroom, just outside of the football stadium. He lets go of my arm and presses his hands on either side of me. I realize that this situation probably isn't going to end well, but my anxiety begins to subside. As close as Tad is, he's not touching me anymore.

I can think again.

Feel again.

Pain surges through my arm like a lightning bolt. It was probably there the whole time, but I didn't notice. I'm going to have five little bruises from the pressure of his fingers but I don't move to soothe the throbbing. I hold my ground, fists balled at my sides, and stare up at him.

"I'm not above dragging you into the bathroom, but I don't want to do that. I just need you to go in there with me, Piper." Tad rests his forehead against the wall. His breath loud and shaky beside my ear. "A thousand dollars," he says suddenly, turning his head, begging me with his eyes to concede. "Walk in there with me. Please. You have to. "

If my heart wasn't already racing, it would be. That's a lot of money, enough for a ticket out of town and a few nights at a cheap motel. It's not nearly enough to pay my bio-mom's debts, but it would put a dent in it and maybe keep everyone off my back a little longer.

I don't know though. Whatever rumor is bound to start about me would be gone in eight short weeks, but this situation doesn't feel right. Something's off. "I need that money. More than you can imagine, but no."

Tad beats his fist on the wall beside me. I flinch, but he's so lost in himself he doesn't seem to notice. "What the fuck, Piper? I've offered you ten times more than your worth. If you don't go in there, I'm gonna be..." He shakes his head.

"I don't want—"

Tad turns to me again, this time crashing his lips onto mine. He tastes like cigarettes and tuna fish, two things I hate. His hands push into my hair, tangling and pulling my roots. Bile creeps up my throat.

I don't want this.

I don't want him.

No! I bite down on the tongue that's invaded my mouth and press my palms to Tad's chest, pushing as hard as I can. He stumbles back a step and stares at me, wide eyed, apparently shocked that I rejected him.

"You bitch!" He raises his hand and slapping me across the face. "You don't want to do this the easy way, fine. We can do it—!"

"Hey!" A deep voice booms from my right. A wide, tall body comes out of nowhere, physically shielding me with its massive frame while a hand shoves Tad's shoulder.

Tad loses his balance and stumbles a step to the right. "The fuck you want, Montgomery?"

Rex Montgomery—owner of said voice—reaches behind him and puts a protective hand on my hip. With everything that's happening, my brain doesn't seem to register the touch. It can't, it's too stunned that *he* of all people came to my rescue.

I mean, the man is a living work of art. At six-foot-four, Rex towers over damn near everyone at St. A's. Teachers included. It's a known fact that he played ice hockey at his last school, and rumor has it he's already been drafted to go semi-pro next season. Needless to say, every inch of him is carved from gold. Not really, but I hear his muscles are drool worthy. Add to that near perfect body a strong jawline and an angled nose. Yeah, girls swoon just from hearing his name. I'll admit, I might be one of them, sometimes, but never in public.

"Leave her alone," he growls.

Tad snorts. "That's cute. You sticking up for the trash. This bitch doesn't belong here, Rex. All girls like her are good for is a quick lay."

"Fuck you," I yell. Rex squeezes my hip, probably trying to be reassuring. Oddly enough, it works. A calm settles over me, releasing an unexpected smile.

What the heck is happening right now?

"Tell you what, you can take her into the boys bathroom first. When you're done I'll do my thing with her in the girl's. My treat, man."

Without warning Rex swings, catching Tad off guard with a right hook to the eye. Rex moves like a shark. Agile. Quick. And with precision. He swings again, hitting with enough force to knock Tad back a step.

I stand there like an idiot. Mouth open. Eyes gaping as if this is the first time I've witnessed two boys throw down. I've seen fights before. Hell, my tattoo artist runs a backyard fight club once a month that once upon a time I used to go to.

But this is different.

The rage in Rex's eyes is unlike anything I've ever seen. It's terrifying and unbelievably hot at the same time. I couldn't tear my gaze away even if I tried.

Tad grunts and lunges forward, hitting Rex in the stomach with his shoulder, but he barely moves. Rex punches him in the side, once, twice, then slams Tad's face onto his knee.

Tad falls to the ground, panting, blood seeping from his nose and a cut on his brow. He took a hell of a beating, and I have no clue how he's still conscious. Must be all that practice getting his ass handed to him on the football field. Defeated, he holds a hand up in surrender.

All of this is going on and I'm over here, less than three feet from the action, fighting the urge to jump up and down like a freaking cheerleader. Something has to be wrong with me today. I've never been the preppy ra-ra type. I'm more of a glare at you from a distance kind of girl. But watching Rex kick Tad's ass has me feeling some kind of way.

"Since you were too stupid to listen the first time, I'll tell you again. Piper's closed for business," Rex growls. "You will not stop her in the hallway or corner her when she's alone. Your days of talking to or thinking about Piper are done. If I find you in the same room as her outside of class, I'll kick your ass three ways from Sunday. Got it?"

All the bubbly feelings I had watching Rex kick Tad's ass disappear. Reality smacks me in the face with a horde of questions.

What does Rex mean by the first time?

Is he the reason everyone has left me alone the last few weeks?

What the hell is going on!?

Tad spits blood onto the ground and nods. "Got it."

"Good," Rex says rising to his feet. "Now get the hell out of here before I beat the living shit out of you again."

I watch Rex while he watches Tad walk away, guarding me until that low-life is out of sight.

Rex turns. His dark brown hair, short on the sides but long enough to run your fingers through on top, blows in the rare Florida breeze like a damn shampoo commercial. Under normal circumstances I'd make fun of him for it but I'm too stunned to speak. My mind's still tripping over the fact that *he* saved me. That he touched me and that my pulse is racing faster than a greyhound from the way he is still looking at me.

"Are you okay?" Rex takes my chin between his thumb and forefinger to examine my face. My breath catches. Not because I'm anxious, but because the feeling of impending doom isn't there. There's no tightness in my chest or nervous shakes. No needles shooting down my spine or fuzziness in my head. Instead, there's an electric current pulsating between us that I've never felt before, similar to my anxiety needles yet different.

"I'm fine." I'm not fine. My skin's on fire, the space between my legs aches, and I'm a confused mess. Rex is the first person to touch me this year who doesn't send my body into shock. His skin on mine should ignite a catalyst of crippling reactions. Instead, heat spreads from my cheeks down to my core. Awakening parts of me I thought died long ago.

Rex drops his hand. Deep blue's study me, combing over every feature, making my insecurities bubble up. The bags under my eyes. The scars on my arms, some hidden beneath a colorful tattoo, others still visible to all who look beyond the dozen rubber bracelets.

"Wanna get out of here?" He asks with zero traces of hidden innuendo.

Another first. The only time guys—who aren't the Harris twins—talk to me is to ask for a favor. An unfortunate hazard of my reputation.

Please don't let Rex ask a favor.

"Piper?"

Shit. I must have zoned out. No, I don't want to leave with you because I don't know what's going on with me! I shake my head, hoping I didn't actually say those words aloud.

Rex smiles revealing two deep, beautiful dimples.

The overwhelming need to have his hands on my body consumes me. Tears prick the back of my eyes again because for the first time in a year I want to be held. What's worse, I want to be comforted by him — the hot almost stranger who saved me.

I hate it.

I like it.

I don't know how to take it. I've gone so long learning how to cope with the anxiety of unwanted touch that I forgot how to react when it's desired. I look up at Rex, feeling like a complete idiot, unsure of what to do next. Should I say thank you? Is that enough? I mean, what he just did, saving me, is huge!

"Can I walk you inside? I'm sure Cooper wouldn't want you by yourself after that bullshit. And I..." he rubs at the back of his neck. "I don't want to leave you alone. You know, in case Tad comes back."

"Okay." My voice cracks, sounding nothing like its usual calm, collected self. Rex steps closer and tucks me under his arm. There's a bubble in my chest but I can still breathe. Still function.

I think I'm nervous.

Go figure. The hottest guy in school that I'll *never* have a chance with is ushering me inside and *now* my brain starts to act like a teenage girl. If I can't get this under control, I'm screwed.

Rex angles his body to shield me from eyes that might be watching as we cross the parking lot. The smell of musk and clean linen swirl in my head. It's delicious. I sniff again, committing the scent to memory because the likelihood that I'll be this close to him again is slim to none. Even if Rex can touch me without causing a debilitating panic attack, handsome, popular guys don't actually like girls like me. They just like the way we make them feel.

Thank you

To me, this is the hardest part of the book to write because there are so many wonderful people who help make each story come alive and every time I get to this page, my mind goes blank.

First and foremost, I want to thank my BFF Alexandria James, who is the backbone to every story I write. She lets me throw ideas at her and takes them in stride, half the time having no clue which book I'm talking about or who has been rattling my mind. Without her The Lost Darling would be sitting in a file along with the other four half-written stories I haven't finished.

My mom is always on this list because not only is she my biggest fan, she is my always the first set of eyes on every story.

A special thank you to Alyssa Friess for being my star beta reader. I had five people sign up and she was the only one to give me feedback. So thank you!

Thank you to Ashleigh Blakely for volunteering to be my final eyes before publication. Her attention to detail is immaculate.

To my editor Beth at Magnolia Author Services I found you four books ago and as long as you want me I will forever be a repeat customer. (Indie authors...if your looking she's the shit!)

To my kick-ass PA, Becky... you make it possible for me to focus on writing. Without you I'd be a squirrel of half thoughts, open giveaways, and with a dead Facebook group.

To my husband who says he wants nothing to do with my books but hounds me when I haven't written anything in a week... I love you.

To the bloggers and bookstagrammers who bring my stories to the world. You are amazing! I cannot begin to express how grateful to you I am.

To everyone I'm sure to have forgotten because I'm Dory's second cousin twice removed and feel like I'd forget my head if it wasn't attached.

Finally, I'd like to thank my readers. Every time you open one of my books, you make my dream come true.

Thank you.

Xoxo

Bailey

About Bailey

Bailey Black broke into the writing world as contemporary romance author Bailey B, but as she dove into the fantasy world she decided she needed a last name. She loves reading, hanging out with her family, and tries to keep up with all eight of her pets.

CPSIA information can be obtained
at www.ICGtesting.com
Printed in the USA
JSHW022030060922
30069JS00003B/149

9 798218 054670